# Cowboy

## Melissa Stevens

TNT Publications

The Ride with Me books are for Daniel.
Twenty-seven years is a lifetime. It hasn't always been easy.
Sometimes it's been harder than you can imagine. We've
shared tears and laughter, blessings and loss. But it's always
been worth it.
I'm looking forward to twenty-seven more, and all that they
bring us.
You're the only one I want to Ride with Me.

# Contents

# 1

Cowboy clenched his teeth as he watched the hot little blonde across the room. He hadn't wanted to come out tonight, but he'd let Deacon talk him into it. 'Relaxing' and 'destressing' Deke had called it.

Cowboy didn't really find blasting music and gyrating bodies in a hot, sweaty crowd all that relaxing, but he'd gone along with it because he'd needed time with his brother and since when had he turned down a chance to pick up some chick and get laid?

Well, aside from the last six months. He'd struggled for the last six months to hold the Kings of Destruction together. They'd lost a quarter of their membership since he'd taken over. Part of them to prison, which was why he'd taken over, and the rest following the men who'd been stripped of their patches for misuse of club resources.

He pushed thoughts of the club, and his struggles with it out of his mind as he watched the woman take another drink then flit out to the dance floor. He'd had his eye on her for most of the last hour.

"Looks like you got your eye on someone there, brother," Deke shouted over the music.

"You paid any attention to her?" Cowboy tilted his head toward the blonde.

"Which one?" Deke turned to watch the dance floor as he picked up his glass of Jim Beam.

"The blonde dancing like she's hunting for the last available dick on earth."

"I hadn't noticed, but she should be an easy pick up if that's what you're looking for."

Cowboy didn't say anything, just narrowed his eyes as another man approached her. They spoke for a minute, but in contrast to what he'd thought about the way she danced, she turned him away. The expression on his face made Cowboy think she hadn't been nice about it.

"Well, that's interesting. I thought she was looking for a dick to jump on." Deke tilted his head to one side as he continued watching the woman, obviously seeing what Cowboy had.

"Maybe not. I wonder what's up." Cowboy continued to watch her, as well as the guy she'd brushed off.

A few songs later, Deke jumped then pulled out his phone.

"Crap. I have to go."

"Need help?"

"Nah, I got it. Besides. It looks like you've got a lead on some pussy."

Cowboy barely reined in the urge to roll his eyes.

"You okay here or should I send someone to cover your back?"

That he couldn't let go. Cowboy turned and pinned his brother with a don't make me kill you look until Deke held his hands up in surrender, then shoved his chair back and left.

Cowboy watched the blonde for a while longer. Watched several more men approach her and were rebuffed. He shook his head and decided she must not be looking to hook up, more likely she was coming off a breakup, possibly a bad one. Chances were she was cutting loose and not looking to go home with anyone but herself; unless someone took advantage of her.

In his peripheral vision, Cowboy noticed two of the men she'd turned down standing near a tall table, chatting while both men kept looking back at her. Something about the way they moved and the looks they shot her set off warning bells in his mind.

He abandoned his table, went to the bar, and ordered an orange juice. Anyone who saw him with it would assume it was a screwdriver, but he wanted to be clear headed. Especially if these two were up to what he suspected they were. He kept his eyes on her on the dance floor, but eased his way to where the two men still stood, eyeing her.

The booming music made it next to impossible to hear everything they were saying unless he was standing at the table with them, and maybe not even then. But he caught a word here and there. Things like stuck up and asking for it. No way these two were up to anything good.

Cowboy knew better than to try to pick up the girl, even if she were interested, he wasn't into taking advantage of drunk women. Instead, he hung around until she was ready to leave, then caught her just outside the door as she staggered to the wall beside the door and paused, bracing herself against the wall as she regained her balance before taking a few more steps.

Something wasn't right. Had she drunk enough she could barely walk, or had she been slipped something? He stepped heavily so she wouldn't be startled by his arrival as he came up behind her.

"You look like you could use some help. Let me help you get home." He was careful not to touch her as he offered her a hand.

She paused and blinked at him. Cowboy wasn't sure he'd managed to not startle her, but she didn't panic. He gave her credit for that.

"I don't know if I should," her words slurred.

Almost certainly too much to drink. It was possible she'd been slipped something, and he wouldn't put it past the pair who were so pissed at her, but he didn't think so.

"I just want to make sure you make it home. Where do you live?"

She blinked big eyes at him and even in the dim lighting around the club he could tell they were a pale blue.

"I'm around the corner and just down the street."

"Can you walk, or should I get my truck?"

"I can—" she hiccuped, "I can walk." She took a few more staggering steps then stopped again, her shoulder hitting the wall.

Cowboy shook his head. "Here, let me help you." He took her arm gently and helped her walk a little more steadily.

He asked directions several times, then when they got to her apartment door, he waited while she tried to get the key in the lock for what seemed like forever before he asked for the keys and let them in.

"Where's the bedroom?" he asked once they were inside, and the door was closed.

"This way." She flung an arm to the left.

"Come on. Let's get you into bed before you pass out." He walked her down the short hall where she all but nose-dived into the bed.

Cowboy shook his head as he pulled off her boots, then pulled the blanket up over her snoring body. Looking around he found a trash can not far away and moved it to beside the bed in case she got sick. Then he left a glass of water, and a couple of Tylenol he found on the kitchen counter on the table next to the bed.

He carried her keys back into the kitchen and found a notebook there, where she was working on a grocery list. He pulled a clean sheet from the notebook and wrote a quick note.

*Sleep well,*

*Cowboy.*

He added his phone number, put her keys on the paper and let himself out, making sure he locked the door on his way out.

# 2

Sunlight seemed to stab through her closed eyelids, that and a pounding head woke Ava. She rolled over, trying to get away from the light, and her stomach lurched. Where was she? She searched her memory, trying to figure out what happened.

The last thing she remembered was turning down yet another of several men who thought a woman out dancing alone must be looking for a guy to pick her up. The last one hadn't been nice about it and had called her a stuck-up bitch. He'd hurt her feelings, but she knew she didn't have to put out just because she felt like dancing and some stranger took it as an invitation.

Her stomach began to settle and after a moment she risked opening her eyes. A glass of water sat on her nightstand. Where had that come from? She didn't remember leaving one there. There was something beside it.

Ava lifted her head to take a closer look then had to close her eyes as the motion made the jackhammer working on her head go into overdrive. When the ache in her head had eased enough that she could open her eyes, she realized what she hadn't been able to see well was two Tylenol capsules. She sent a silent thank you to her drunk self for thinking to put these out. But if she'd set them out, why hadn't she taken them?

It took her a moment to sit up enough she could take the pills and sip the water. Carefully at first, making sure it didn't upset her stomach, then faster once she decided her stomach would handle it.

She sat, eyes closed for several minutes trying to gather the will to get up and go find something to eat. The thought of food set her stomach churning again, but she knew she needed to eat something.

How had she managed to get her boots off and neat beside the bed, but leave her clothes on?

Her first stop was the bathroom, where she sat on the floor for a few minutes, half afraid she was going to be sick. After a bit she was able to get her stomach under control. Then she staggered into the kitchen. Why had getting drunk sounded so good?

She was old enough to know better, or at least she should have been. If she hadn't married before she was old enough to drink and stayed away from alcohol because Hank had insisted it wasn't fitting that his wife might be seen with alcohol, then she might have enough experience to know better.

In the kitchen she opened the fridge and looked inside. Neither juice nor milk held any appeal. And she didn't want to cook. What did she have that she could just eat. Hadn't she gotten crackers when she'd been shopping a few days ago?

She closed the fridge, went to the cabinet, and found the box of Ritz. She opened a tube while turning around and leaning her butt against the counter. Popping the first cracker in her mouth she closed her eyes and prayed it would settle her stomach. Eyes still closed, she shook her head and tried to remember the last time she'd prayed. Probably almost a year ago. Before she'd caught Hank in the office with his secretary slipping her something that sure as hell hadn't been the holy ghost.

Ava pushed the memory of Hank and all that had come before and after that moment, from her mind. She wondered again how she'd gotten home. After a couple crackers, her stomach seemed to have calmed down. It was probably time to think about finding more to eat.

Opening her eyes, she spotted her keys on the counter. She didn't remember leaving them there. She always hung them on the hook at the end of the bar. Ava picked up the keys and stared at them for a moment trying to remember putting them there, but came up with nothing so she hung them up. It wasn't until she set the tube of crackers on the counter that she realized the keys had been sitting on a piece of paper. With a frown she picked it up and read the brief note.

Cowboy? Who was Cowboy? She hoped he wasn't one of the men who had been so ugly to her last night.

*Oh my God.*

There had been someone in her apartment last night. What had he done while he was here? Her body flashed cold, and her knees went weak. She sank to the floor. Had they had sex? Had he raped her?

Wait. She'd woken nearly fully dressed. She looked down at herself. Nothing seemed buttoned wrong. Her bra was still in place and remembering her trip to the bathroom a few minutes ago, so was her underwear. Was it possible she'd been redressed?

Of course, but who went to that much trouble once they had what they wanted? And what kind of person would do that to a woman then leave their phone number?

Thinking back over everything she'd seen and done since she'd woken up, she remembered the water and the pills. Maybe she hadn't left them for herself? Getting out of bed she'd kicked over the trash can. She couldn't recall putting it beside the bed. Maybe because she hadn't?

Ava didn't know how long she sat there, wondering what kind of guy would take a woman home, put her to bed, make sure she had meds then leave. When she got to her feet, she went to check the door, hoping he hadn't left it unlocked. Sure enough. It was locked.

She checked her pocket for her phone but didn't find it. Had she lost it last night? If this mysterious Cowboy had brought her home and put her in bed, she couldn't imagine him stealing her phone, especially having left his number.

It took a few minutes for her hangover clouded brain to register, but she went back in the bedroom and peeled back the blankets. There she found her phone, halfway under her pillow.

Ava knew what she needed to do, but couldn't bring herself to do it, not yet. Her stomach grumbled, reminding her that all she'd put in it was a glass of water and a few crackers. She needed something more than that. She'd call this Cowboy person after she ate.

# 3

Cowboy sat at his desk in the office of his shop drawing up a design a client from out of state wanted for a bike when his phone rang. Distracted, he didn't even glance at the screen, just hit the button on the screen to answer, letting the headset that had been streaming music to block out the noise in the shop switch over to the call.

"This is Cowboy."

"Um, Hi," a hesitant woman's voice said. "My name's Ava and I don't know if I've got the right person," she let out a nervous laugh, "but I think you brought me home last night."

Those words pulled him out of his distraction.

"I'm sorry. Did you say your name is Ava?"

"I did. Did I not tell you that last night? I hate to admit it, but I have no memory of you." She paused and he gave her a moment in case she wanted to say more, but she didn't.

"Not surprising. You were pretty shitfaced last night. I hope you're feeling okay this morning."

"As good as can be expected, I guess. I won't be doing that again any time soon."

"Which part?" He couldn't help the teasing note in his voice and hoped she wouldn't be offended by it. "You looked like you were having fun, and I'll never support giving up fun." He leaned back in the swivel chair, stretching out the kinks from having been over the desk, then getting a little more comfortable.

"No, I'm not giving up the fun part, but drinking till I don't know where I am or who brought me home? That's not going to happen again. I just hope I wasn't too stupid."

"I'll agree with not letting yourself get so far gone you don't know where you are, or who you are with, but you weren't totally stupid. I watched as several men hit on you and you turned them down. I don't know why you let me take you home, but I was the only guy you didn't refuse all night long. Maybe because I wasn't hitting on you. I just wanted to make sure you made it home."

"Thank you for that. I can't say that enough."

"No need. I just did what was right."

"Did you leave water and Tylenol beside the bed? I thought at first that I had and just didn't remember it, but that was before I realized you'd brought me home."

"That was me. We got you home, you went into the bedroom and passed out as soon as your head hit the pillow. I wanted you to be comfortable, so I took off your boots, but didn't want to intrude so I left your clothes on. If I'd thought about it before you made it into bed, I would have had you drink water first, then you wouldn't feel so bad this morning. Since I was too late for that, I put the water next to the bed."

"Does water really make you feel better?" She sounded doubtful.

"It does. The hangover is mostly from dehydration. If you drink water while you're drinking, it's not so bad. But I have to admit, even knowing better, I still sometimes forget." He wondered how she didn't know this. He would have guessed her age at thirty at least. Surely, this hadn't been her first time drunk?

She groaned. "I don't think I'll be drinking much in the near future."

"I wouldn't say you need to give up drinking, not if you enjoyed it, but maybe next time go out with a friend. Someone to help make sure you make it home safe."

"I planned to last night, but she cancelled last minute. One of her kids got sick. It was just around the corner, and I didn't see the harm. I see why people go out in pairs and groups now."

A glance at his watch told him he needed to get busy. The client he was doing this sketch for was in town and wanted to see it in just over an hour.

"I'm glad you're not feeling too bad, but I need to get back to work. I've got a meeting soon and I need to be ready."

"Oh, I'm sorry. I didn't think. I assumed you're off today like I am. I'll let you go but really quick I wanted to take you to lunch, as a thank you for bringing me home."

"You don't have to do that."

"But I want to. I don't know many people who would do something like that, and lunch is the least I can do."

"All right but I'm busy today. I can do tomorrow if that works for you?"

"I can do that. Where do you want to go?"

Cowboy named a diner he liked but didn't get to often, she didn't know where it was but said she'd figure it out and she'd meet him there tomorrow, then rang off.

The music turned back on in the headset he wore, and Cowboy turned his attention back to the sketch he was working on. He was running out of time and as much as he'd wanted to keep talking to Ava, this was more important.

# 4

A va walked into the little diner and looked around. How would she know if he was already here? She hadn't realized until this moment she had no idea what he looked like. It felt like everyone was staring because she had been standing there an inordinate length of time when she spotted a man near the back waving at her.

She smiled and made her way back to where he sat, weaving in between tables. She took her time so she could get a good look at him. He was handsome, a red head going gray, but he didn't look old enough to be that gray. It was hard to tell while he was seated but he looked like he was in good shape. At least his t-shirt clung to him in all the right ways. As she got closer, she couldn't help but notice his bright green eyes that seemed to speak to her despite his not saying anything yet.

"Are you Cowboy?" she asked as she got close enough to be heard without raising her voice. She felt dumb enough using what was obviously a nickname without knowing him, or at least she hoped it was a nickname.

"I am," he said with a nod. "I'm glad to see you more aware of your surroundings." He stood and offered her a hand. She took it and shook it. "Have a seat." He motioned to the other side of the table.

Ava pulled out the chair and tucked her skirt under as she sat. Cowboy took his seat again as soon as she did. The waitress appeared next to the table before she had a chance to say anything. The name tag on her shirt read 'Betsy'.

"I know you just got here, sugar, but any idea what you'd like to drink?"

Ava blinked, not having been ready to order yet. Coffee? Didn't sound good, she'd had enough already.

"Water, please."

"No problem, you want lemon with that?"

"No thanks."

When Betsy left, Ava took a deep breath and forced herself not to bite her lip, no matter how badly she wanted to.

"Thanks again for the night before last." She shook her head. "It was a stupid thing to do, I know. I wish I could say I didn't know better, but I did. I knew I should have gone with someone, but I just moved to town, and I only know a couple of people. They were busy and I was tired of waiting for life to happen to me." She didn't know why she felt like she needed to explain her actions to him, yet found herself doing it just the same.

"Hey, I get wanting to cut loose once in a while. Next time you want to go out and don't have anyone to watch your back, I'd be happy to go with you, if only to make sure you make it home safely. No strings attached."

"That's a very generous offer." She didn't know what else to say, not now. She picked up her menu and took her time deciding what she wanted. She couldn't help but notice Cowboy never touched his menu.

By the time Betsy returned with her water, Ava knew what she wanted. Betsy took their orders then left.

"Where do you get a name like Cowboy?" she asked before he had a chance to ask about her.

He chuckled.

"Rest assured, it's not my given name. I've had several ask that. It's a nickname. Given to me a long time ago by my club."

"Club?" What kind of club gave you nick names? She knew a lot of men ended up with them in the military, but a club?

"I'm part of a riding club, have been for years."

Now she was even more confused.

"Riding? Like horses?" What else could he mean? But why would a bunch of people riding horses dub one of them Cowboy?

"Not exactly, I ride motorcycles. Well, one mainly, but I have been known to ride others."

"Oh." Ava tried to remember everything she'd ever heard about motorcycle riders and motorcycle clubs. Nothing good came to mind. What she remembered hearing didn't line up with what she knew of Cowboy's character, perhaps what she'd heard was wrong? Over the last year she'd learned a lot of what she'd thought she knew or had been told was wrong.

She'd learned that people who were supposed to be trustworthy, weren't, and now it seemed the people she'd been taught to stay away from, to fear, might be the most trustworthy of all.

"Not what you expected?"

"Honestly? No, but probably not for the reason you think." She shook her head, trying to decide how much she wanted to share. After a moment she took a deep breath and began, "I'm learning that a lot of things I thought I knew aren't what I'd been taught. This is just another."

He cocked one brow and watched her for a moment. "Just like that?"

"Just like that. It might be harder if this was the first, or even the second revelation, but it's just one in what's become a long stream of lies I believed to be fact." She couldn't help a wry smile as she remembered some of the things she'd been told and believed, but now knew to be false.

"It sounds like you've been through a lot."

"You could say that." She didn't want to go into it, so she changed the subject. "You been in Dickenson long?"

"Close to ten years. You?"

"About three months."

"So, you're a newbie. Can I ask what brought you to our neck of the woods?"

"Like I said, I've had a lot of changes recently. I wanted to be closer to family. My brother and his wife live here, so I came here to be closer to him."

"Nice. Mind if I ask if you've found a job yet?"

"I have, or I'd probably still be living with Aaron. That's my brother." She picked up her glass and took a sip, using it as an excuse to gather her thoughts. "I work at the bank on Villard."

"A manager?"

Ava shook her head. "I wish. Actually, no I don't. I don't have enough experience for something like that. I've only been working again for the last few months, there's no way I could manage something like managing a bank, or pretty much anywhere else, except maybe a church. I've done that enough I could manage, but who's going to hire me for that?"

Cowboy tilted his head and watched her.

"Manage a church? Are you some kind of pastor?"

Ava couldn't help but laugh. "No, but my ex-husband is. I was nothing but a dutiful wife. And even that wasn't enough." She shook her head and met his gaze. "Enough of that. I'm not here to tell you about my mistakes. Tell me more about you. You said you're part of a motorcycle club, am I calling it the right thing?" At his nod she continued, "Do you do anything else?"

"I do. I design and build custom bikes."

"Oh, I didn't know there was a big bike market in North Dakota." She hadn't noticed any bike paths. Maybe she was looking on the wrong streets?

"Bigger than you think. On top of that, we're only about three hours from Sturgis, so we get a lot of traffic around the Rally."

Ava's face heated as she realized he hadn't been talking about bicycles, but motorcycles again. It wasn't until he'd said Sturgis that it had even occurred to her. She wanted to hide her face in her hands, but forced herself to keep her hands in her lap, at least for now.

A slow smile crept across his face. "You were thinking bicycles, weren't you?"

She nodded, unable to meet his gaze.

"A lot of people do. It amuses me to see how long it takes them to catch on. You were way faster than a lot of people to pick it up. What part made it click?"

"Sturgis. I may be sheltered, but even I've heard of the rally in Sturgis."

"You said you'd just moved here. Do you mind my asking where you came from?"

"Several places, but most recently a small town in Arizona you've probably never heard of."

Cowboy's eyes went wide. "Arizona to North Dakota. I bet this is cold to you, it's got to be more like the winter temperatures down there?"

"It's close. But the winter's there are nice, which is why there are so many winter visitors."

"Winter visitors? That must be a local term. All I've ever heard them called are snowbirds."

Ava laughed again. "We use that too, but sometimes snowbirds is used as a curse by the locals, so winter visitors became the more politically correct term."

A low growl rumbled from him, making her jump.

"Political correctness is going to be the end of us some day. Thankfully, most of the people I deal with don't expect it. Especially from a grizzled old biker." He grinned at her, revealing a straight row of white teeth.

Ava lifted one corner of her lips in a wry half smile. "Politically correct is expected from a pastor's wife. Wouldn't want to anger any member of the congregation. They might leave or, heaven forbid, complain to the conference. That is never a pleasant interaction." She let a small shudder run through her.

"It doesn't sound as if it would be."

"Somehow the subject keeps turning back around to things I'd rather not talk about. I have a question for you, though, if you don't mind."

"Shoot. If it's something I don't want to answer, I'll say so."

"What's it feel like to ride a motorcycle?" It was a dumb question, she knew, but she'd always wanted to know.

"Unbelievable." He chuckled then sat back in his chair to watch her. "I know that's not very descriptive, but riding is impossible to describe." He shook his head. "There's the wind in your face, the feel of the bike beneath you, the sense of freedom."

Ava couldn't help but notice the light in his eyes as he spoke. He might not be able to give a description he believed gave justice to the experience, but she could tell he loved the experience by the way he talked and the glint in his eyes.

She wished she had the nerve to ask for a ride. But he was a stranger, and she'd already imposed enough by his taking her home. This was her saying thank you, not her asking him to do something more for her.

# 5

Cowboy watched Ava and couldn't help but be reminded of Lisa, his younger sister. She was fifteen years his junior, so he remembered her younger years well. At the time he hadn't appreciated her innocent honesty, but now, with more perspective, he wished he'd appreciated it more.

"You said you were married." He paused as the waitress delivered their food then left. Before he had a chance to continue, she spoke up.

"Yes, but I'd rather not talk about that."

"No worries, I just had a question. Any kids?" He hadn't seen any sign of them in her apartment, but maybe whatever had caused the divorce had given her ex-husband custody.

"No," she looked down at her plate, "I wanted them, and we tried, but I could never get pregnant. After years of trying, I wanted to see a doctor, but Hank insisted it was God's will and forbade it." She took a deep breath, straightened her shoulders, and looked up, meeting his gaze. "Looking at how things have turned out, it's probably for the best. Still, I wish I had at least gotten pregnant once. I feel like I'm missing something."

The sadness and loss were apparent on her face. He felt for her. He'd never yearned for kids before, but seeing how badly she did, it made him wonder if maybe he was missing something by not having any. But then, who would he trust to have his child? He hadn't had a relationship that lasted past sunrise in longer than he cared to think about.

"You're still young enough for kids. It's not too late." He was sure she couldn't be more than thirty-two or three, there was still lots of time for her to have children. Hell, more and more women were waiting until after that to even start thinking about them.

"That may be true but look at me. Look at my life now. I'm thirty-five and barely able to support myself. How would I support a kid too? Besides, I'd also have to find a father, or be a single mom and..." She trailed off then shook her head. "No, that's one dream I'm going to have to let go of."

He hated seeing the sad and lost look on her face. It made him want to say he could help, but he bit his tongue. That was a huge thing to volunteer for. And she was a stranger at that, no matter how intriguing.

They ate and chatted, getting to know each other a bit better. But at the end of the meal, Cowboy couldn't help wanting to spend more time with her. Even though he didn't know her well, she intrigued him and for some reason he didn't understand, he felt more at home around her than around most of the people he'd known, aside from his brothers. His Kings of Destruction brothers that was. His only blood brother and he didn't get along. He hadn't even spoken to Terry in over three years.

When Betsy brought the ticket, Cowboy had to stop himself from picking it up. He knew enough about women to know that she would likely get angry if he tried to pay. Especially since she'd told him she was taking him to lunch as a thank you for making sure she got home safe. Still, it irked his sense of right and wrong to let her pick up the tab. Especially after she'd said she was barely able to support herself.

"I've enjoyed this," he said after she'd sent her card with Betsy to pay for their meals. "I'd like to take you out again. This time I'll pay." He smiled, hoping she wouldn't be insulted by his saying he wanted to pay.

"I don't know." Her gaze dropped to her hands. "I don't go out much and when I do, I seem to find trouble. You saw that."

"You didn't find trouble. Trouble could have found you, but I didn't let that happen night before last and I'll do my best to keep it from happening if you'll go out with me. Dinner, maybe a movie, though we could go dancing if you like. I liked watching you dance."

Ava turned pink, as if the memory of her dancing embarrassed her. He didn't know why it should, but then she seemed more repressed, or maybe innocent was the right word, with no alcohol to loosen her inhibitions. It stirred a protective instinct stronger than he could ever recall feeling, even for Lisa when she'd been in school and some asshole had been harassing her.

"I guess it would be okay. When do you want to go out?" She kept her voice soft, and didn't look up at him.

Cowboy wanted to say now. Tonight. But thought that would be too much, too soon for her.

"How about tomorrow night?"

She glanced up at him then back down again. "I can do tomorrow. What should I wear?"

"Want a ride on my bike?" He watched her closely, wanting to read her reaction as well as her words.

The blush from moments before had faded, but she flushed now, and he knew the idea excited her.

"I don't know. Isn't it dangerous?"

"It can be, but I'll make sure nothing happens. It will be fun and one more thing to mark off that bucket list."

Her full lips disappeared as she bit them, obviously trying to screw up the nerve.

"All right. Let's do it." She looked up at him, excitement shining in her eyes. "What should I wear?"

"Jeans, a jacket of some kind and the boots you had on last night would be perfect. If you have a purse, something with a long strap that can go across your body works best." Well, second best, after a backpack, but most women wouldn't carry a backpack in place of a purse so there was no point suggesting it.

"Anything else I should know?"

He scanned her from head to toe, looking for things that wouldn't be safe on the bike. "You can pull your hair back, but keep it low, so a braid or low ponytail, or the helmet will be painful very quickly."

"Oh, good to know." She tapped fingertips against her thumb in succession, as if counting something, then spoke again, still focusing on her hands. "Let me make sure I have it all. Casual dress, but warm. Boots, long strap on the purse, hair up and low. Right?" She looked up at him, her eyes a light with excitement.

"Warm but layers, because you might get warm at the theater and want to take it off. And you're hair doesn't have to be up, but if it is, it needs to be low. I like your hair. It looks like every strand is a slightly different color, so you can never be sure what color it really is." He resisted the urge to reach out and see if it was as soft as it looked.

If he got his way, he'd have a chance to feel it soon enough. Same with her lips. They were full and plump, and he ached to know what she tasted like, but it was way too soon. They hadn't even had a single date.

"Thank you." She looked uncomfortable talking about her hair, and he wondered why, but she kept talking. "And thank you for agreeing to this." She motioned to the table between them.

He started to tell her it was nothing, he was just doing what any decent person would do, but she cut him off.

"We know it's not what anyone would do. All we have to do is turn on the news to know that. You did something big, at least to me. I want you to know I appreciate it."

"Then you're welcome." He didn't know what else to say.

"Now, I have to go. I have a few errands to run, then Aaron, my brother, is expecting me for dinner. I know he's got a lot going on, but he's made a point to have me for dinner every Sunday since I got to town. He's trying to help as much as he can." She gathered her phone and looked around the table top to make sure she hadn't left anything else, then stood. Cowboy stood along with her, while she dropped her phone into her bag.

"Let me walk you out."

"You don't have to do that."

"I'm headed out anyway, it's no big deal. Plus, it gives me just a couple minutes longer with you." He quirked one side of his mouth into a smirk.

"Then thank you." Ava lifted her purse strap onto her shoulder then turned for the door.

# 6

"How was your week?" Aaron asked as they sat down to eat at the small square dinner table in their house.

She had wondered why such a small table, were they not planning on a family?

"It was good. Work all week then I went out night before last." Ava deliberately didn't tell her brother about drinking too much or not knowing how she'd gotten home. "I met someone too. We have a date tomorrow night."

"That's wonderful. Are you ready to move on?" Belinda asked as she forked a couple slices of roast chicken onto her plate then passed the platter to Ava.

"I'm ready to forget what an ass I married and learn to live again." She didn't know if she was ready to move on, as Belinda put it, but she was ready to learn what she'd missed for the last fifteen years.

"I think that's a good attitude. But you need to be careful. Like any city, there are some," Aaron paused as if trying to find the right word, "less than desirable sorts of people. Getting mixed up with them could get you hurt, and I don't just mean break your heart. I love you, sis. I don't want to see you hurt anymore. You've been through enough." He picked up the next dish, scooped some mashed potatoes onto his plate and handed the bowl to Belinda.

"Thank you. I love you too. And I'm not going to do anything stupid." She mentally added nothing more stupid than she'd done Friday night. "But I'm going to stop letting fear hold me back. Especially fear of other people's opinions."

"That's good. I knew there was something off about Hank, but I didn't know that he was browbeating you that way or what he was up to. I would have tried something to help you get out of the situation."

"I know. I don't know that I would have listened if anyone had told me, but there was no denying it when I walked in on him introducing Andrea to more than the holy ghost."

Aaron closed his eyes and seemed to freeze. "I really wish you'd stop saying it like that. It's hard to keep a straight face about something so serious when you put it that way."

Belinda giggled. "But it's funny."

Ava sent a small smile to her sister-in-law. "The whole situation isn't funny, I know that. But I do what I can to keep a positive outlook on life. I could put it any number of ways that would get the point across, but he chose to live his life at my expense, so I see nothing wrong with finding a little amusement at his." She shrugged.

"I don't know. It just seems a bit..." Aaron paused, looking for the right word, "sacrilegious."

"And screwing his secretary on his desk inside the church wasn't?" Ava countered. It wasn't that she had turned her back on the church. But she was currently on what she considered a break while she tried to find meaning in her life again. Did she still believe? In her heart, yes. But it was difficult to get past the anger at this moment. She had no doubt she'd be back. She just didn't know when.

"Okay, fine then. Let's talk about something more pleasant. You said you have a date, what's his name? I might know him."

For some reason she didn't want to tell Aaron and Belinda. Not that she didn't trust them, but she didn't want to potentially jinx what may or may not happen.

"Not important, and I'd rather not know if you know him, not yet. We're just getting to know each other and having a little fun. If it gets more serious, I'll let you know, then you can share what you might know. How was your week? Anything fun happen?"

He narrowed his eyes at her for a moment then went back to eating. "The most fun thing that happened to me today was we got in a new car, several actually but there's one in particular that I think won't last long on the lot."

Ava let her brother talk, she knew it didn't take much to get him to talking about work, not that she really cared. Car sales, yawn. She loved the time she got to spend with Aaron and Belinda, but sometimes she wished he didn't have to act like such a big brother. Even if that was exactly what he was.

After dinner, Ava helped Belinda clean up and do the dishes, then she spent a while visiting with Aaron before going home. Exhausted from her partying and the recovery, she went to bed early so she could get up for work the next morning.

***

The morning part of her day went fast. There was customer after customer and by the time her lunch arrived, Ava was glad to get off her feet for a few minutes. She ate and looked at what movies were playing locally, wondering what they were going to see. She didn't even know where the movie theater was here.

The rest of her shift didn't go so quickly, partly because she was eager to get home and get ready for the date. Ava didn't know which had her more excited. Seeing Cowboy or finally having the chance to ride a motorcycle. Her stomach flip-flopped at the idea. She was a bit nervous, but she trusted him to keep her safe.

By the time five o'clock rolled around, she was all but bouncing out of her skin with excitement. At home, she hurried inside and changed out of her work clothes, sliding into her jeans, and pulling on a tank top, then a blouse to cover her arms. Pulling her denim jacket from the closet, she carried it into the front room with her where she put on the boots she'd worn to the bar, as recommended.

By the time Cowboy knocked on her door, she'd been dressed and ready for twenty minutes, and spent the last fifteen fussing with her hair, and second guessing her choice of tops. She opened the door for him, and his gaze scanned her from head to toe then back up again.

"You look great. I can't wait to spend some time with you. I have a couple questions, would you rather go to the movie here in town, or go to dinner in Bismarck?"

Ava frowned, not sure which option she should take.

"Is there some reason for the change?"

"I wasn't thrilled with the options when I looked at what was playing here, but I don't want to cut the night short. My first thought was to take you to Bismarck for a movie, but I don't want to keep you out too late with work tomorrow."

She tilted her head to one side and watched him for a moment.

"How about dinner and something different. Maybe bowling, tonight? Then, if we want to do this again, we can hit a movie in Bismarck over the weekend?" She tried to keep her tone friendly and hopeful without letting how badly she wanted him to agree leak into her voice.

"Bowling?" he quirked one eyebrow and looked at her from the corner of his eye.

"It doesn't have to be that. It was just a suggestion for something other than driving all that way tonight." Her mind raced, trying to come up with other options.

"When's the last time you went bowling?"

She blinked as her mind went back to what he hadn't seemed interested in.

"Years. Not sure why I even suggested it other than I see the bowling alley on my way home every night."

"Let's do it." He grinned at her like it was a wonderful idea. They have food too, that I hear is pretty good. If you're not too hungry yet we can bowl for a bit, then see if they have anything we want to eat. If you decide you'd rather eat somewhere else, we can do that too."

"Are you sure?"

"Hell yeah. Let's do it. You ready to go? You need to grab anything different or extra to go bowling, different socks maybe?"

She tried remembering what they'd done the last time she'd been bowling and couldn't remember much, other than rented shoes and sliding on the floor.

"I'm good. Ready whenever you are."

"Then come on. I brought an extra helmet. I want you to feel safe."

They left, Ava making sure to lock up on their way out, then he led her to his motorcycle.

Ava almost stopped and stared when she caught sight of his motorcycle. It was bigger than she expected and matte black. That made her think for a moment, when was the last time she saw a matte motorcycle? The ones she could remember were bright and shiny, even the black ones.

They reached the motorcycle, Cowboy opened one of the large boxes to either side of the rear wheel and handed her a helmet. He let her put it on herself, which she appreciated. She fumbled with the strap for a moment, but couldn't figure it out.

"I'm going to need some help with this."

"Here, let me adjust it for you," Cowboy helped her with the strap that went under her chin, then explained how to get on, what to expect while riding, and that she needed to be careful of the pipes or she would get burned.

He climbed on the bike, then had her climb on behind him before starting the bike. Cowboy adjusted her arms round his middle then walked the motorcycle backwards, before he twisted his wrist in an odd movement she didn't understand, and they started moving forward.

Ava had to bite back the squeak of surprise, not that he could have heard it anyway, but she couldn't keep her arms from tightening around him. The way his chest vibrated, she thought he might have laughed, but she couldn't be sure. She was too busy holding on and squeezing her eyes shut.

She did as Cowboy had instructed, leaning with him, and not trying to stay up right when they took turns. She didn't know how far they'd gone but it seemed like they'd been on the bike longer than it took for her to get to work when she'd relaxed enough to open her eyes.

Slowly, she looked around, trying to figure out where they were. Not anywhere she recognized. They were in town, but she couldn't find her way home from here. Panic raced through her for a moment as she wondered if Cowboy had lured her out and had something in mind other than a date, or the kind of date she'd thought he meant.

She must have done something to tip him off to her worry, because he took one hand from the handlebars, patted her hands where they held on around his middle, then reached up and did something with his helmet.

"You all right back there?" Cowboy's voice came through what had to be some kind of radio system in the helmet. She didn't know how to turn hers on so she spoke, hoping he could hear her.

"I'm okay, I think."

"You think?"

She checked his hands, and they were once again on the handlebars.

"I think. I don't know where we are."

"I thought I'd ride for a bit, at least until you relaxed some. You had for a moment then you tensed up again."

"It—" she had to swallow and try again, "it took me a bit to open my eyes, then I realized I don't know where we are."

"And you wondered if I had something nefarious planned. No worries. I don't but you don't know me well enough to know that, not yet. I'll take us back to an area you'll probably know better, then we'll head over to the alley. I just wanted to let you get a feel for the bike, and the short trip to the alley wouldn't do that."

"No, it's okay. I'm enjoying riding. And I'm relaxing more now that I know we can talk to each other. The silence other than the muffled roar of the motorcycle was a little unnerving."

"I didn't even think about that. I'm used to it and find it soothing."

Ava didn't know if she could ever find it soothing, but doubted he'd find the things that she did calming, so decided to let it go. She took a deep breath and forced herself to relax while he steered the motorcycle back onto familiar streets.

# 7

Cowboy pulled the bike into a parking space at the bowling alley and killed the engine. He took off his helmet while he waited for Ava to dismount from behind him, then stepped off himself. He never would have thought of bowling on his own, but now he was looking forward to it.

If nothing else, it would give them time to talk and get to know each other better, plus, he'd get a chance to watch her move. After spending the last half hour with her pressed against his back, he wanted a chance to watch her walk away, but only knowing she would come right back.

They went inside and he asked for a lane, they did the shoe size thing, he paid for their shoes and headed for the lane they'd been assigned. He glanced around, not knowing why he'd expected it to be busier. Only four of the twenty-six lanes were occupied.

"Change shoes or find a ball first?" he asked as he set his rental shoes on one of the seats at their lane.

"I'm going to change shoes, but feel free to choose a ball if you like." She sat and toed off her boots.

Cowboy sat and lifted the hem of his jeans. His boots would take a little more work to get off, since they laced up, so he got to work removing them. He wanted to go with her when she chose her ball, though he couldn't say why.

By the time they'd finished with their shoes, and he'd chosen his ball, she sat at the score keeper seat, working on putting names into the computer. He didn't think they'd had computers for score keeping the last time he'd been in a place like this. It would definitely help keep the score accurate.

"That will be helpful," he motioned to the computer, "I'm not sure I remember how to keep score."

"That's the best part of the newer systems. You don't have to remember all that stuff, add into that that you don't have to worry about math mistakes. It's way easier." Ava finished putting their names into the computer, stood, and smiled at him. "You're first, see?" She pointed to the screen over their lane that had COWBOY in big, animated letters.

He watched her for a moment, taking in the big smile and how it lit her eyes. It made him want to kiss her, but this wasn't the time. Not yet.

Instead, he picked up his ball and headed for the lane, trying to remember how this was done. He took the first throw and watched as his ball rolled down the lane and took out two pins. He thought about making an excuse, but why? He'd already told her he hadn't done this in a long time.

Standing next to the ball return, waiting for his ball, he watched Ava wiggle in her seat, reminding him of an antsy child who had a hard time sitting still. He couldn't help but wonder if she was excited to play, or anxious for some other reason. Hopefully, he'd figure it out in time.

His ball came back. He took it and threw his second frame, not doing any better, but at least he managed to take down the two on the other side of the pins. He turned to Ava and gave her a wry grin.

"Well, there we are. I'm sure you can do better than four."

"We'll see. I'm not as sure as you seem to be." Ava traded places with him, he sat and watched as she stepped up to the line and held her ball. The way her ass swayed as she made tiny steps and shifted her weight while she focused made him want to growl and grab a handful, but this wasn't the place.

He stayed where he was and enjoyed the view. She slowly stepped forward, let the ball swing back, then forward. After she'd released it, she stood frozen at the line for a moment, watching it roll toward the pins. Before it reached them however, Ava started taking small shuffling steps backward. The movement drew his eye to the wiggle of her ass in the snug jeans.

Cowboy had to close his eyes and shift in his seat as his own jeans grew snug.

"Oh!" Ava's voice made him open his eyes again, he found her standing up straight not far from the rearmost line on the floor still staring down the lane. He looked past her to see what had caused her exclamation and found there were only three pins standing.

"That's great! Think you can hit the last ones?"

She turned around and stared at him, wide eyed. He didn't know if the look was because she'd forgotten he was there or was surprised that she'd done so well on her first throw. He didn't care. He loved that look on her, and wondered how many of her other expressions would make him feel the same way.

"I don't know." She slowly shook her head.

"You'll never know if you don't try." He motioned to the ball return where her ball was popping up in the return.

She narrowed her eyes at him then picked up the ball and turned back toward the lane.

He found himself watching her again. He tried to keep his focus on the pins, but as she stepped closer to the line, his gaze went back to her ass and the way those jeans fit. As much as he wanted to watch how well her throw went, he found the way she moved, more tiny steps backwards then freezing again, even more intriguing.

When she spun to look at him, he took the time to glance past her at the pins. She'd knocked down another two pins.

"Nice! And you thought you couldn't do it." He stood, letting her have the seat while he moved to take his turn.

"I didn't but I did get some of them."

"You did better than I did. Don't discount how well you did."

Ava's cheeks turned pink. "Thank you."

She sat and he picked up his ball. He could do this and maybe, just maybe he could keep from embarrassing himself with his score.

They finished the first game. He'd scored 132 to Ava's 197. He felt good about his score and was ready for another game.

"We can go if you want to do something else."

"I'm good. I was going to ask if you want to play another game." He turned and looked around. It took a moment, but he spotted the café, and the menu on the wall above it. "Looks like they've got a pretty good menu. We can have dinner here if you'd like. Or if you'd prefer, we can play another game, or not, and go somewhere else for dinner. I am open for either option."

She watched him a moment before speaking, he got the impression she was trying to figure out if he was telling the truth or not.

"Let's play another game. Give me a few minutes to look at what they've got here then I'll decide if we'll eat here or wait until we're through playing to go get food."

Cowboy couldn't help the grin that spread across his face. He'd gotten past the need to watch her ass as she took her turn, mostly. And they talked a lot as they'd played. She was fun and easy to be around. And she could talk to you. Most of the women he'd spent time around in the last ten plus years only wanted to talk about one thing. What he was going to do to them or what they wanted to do to him. That was his own fault, but he'd lost interest in a quick roll in the hay, then move on to someone new.

"The menu looks good, let's go ahead and eat here," Ava said a few frames later.

"Good, decide what you want, and we can flag down a waitress. Maybe that will give me a chance to redeem myself with a better score."

"I'll decide what I want, but I'm pretty sure we can hit a button to call the waitress." She moved to the control panel for the score computer. "Yep, here's the button. When we're ready we can hit that, and they'll come take our order."

"Wow. I'm glad you're paying attention. I'm still a little blown away by the changes they've made here since the last time I went bowling."

"Was that here?"

"It was, but more years ago than I want to admit to."

"I don't want to admit how long ago it was for me either. Makes me older than I want to admit to."

# 8

"You already told me how old you are, and I still find it hard to believe," Cowboy said.

Ava's face heated. She was too old to be single again, she knew it, but there was no way she was staying with Hank after what she'd walked in on. She pushed that out of her mind and went to step past Cowboy to take her turn, but he caught her with an arm around her waist. She looked up at him, marveling at how someone she barely knew could make heat pool low in her belly.

"You're the best-looking person in this place, thirty-five, twenty-five or eighteen," Cowboy said, keeping his voice low enough so only she could hear him.

Once he'd said that he released her and let her go to take her turn. She stood for a moment facing the lane as she waited for her face to cool and the rush of pleasure that washed through her to fade so she could focus on making her shot.

After throwing the ball, she closed her eyes for a few seconds instead of watching the ball as she usually did. The joy that had come over her at Cowboy's words still raced through her, she didn't even care how well her throw had gone. She opened her eyes, turned, and headed back, assuming she hadn't hit anything because she hadn't heard the ball crash into the pins, but as her gaze landed on Cowboy, she heard it. The ball crashed into the pins. But how? She'd been standing there far longer than it should have taken for the ball to make its way down the lane. She turned to look and had to stop and stare. It was a strike.

She'd been so flustered by what he'd told her, she could barely focus. How on earth had she managed to throw a strike? She blinked to make sure she wasn't seeing things, then turned back to Cowboy.

"That is a strike, right? I'm not seeing things?"

"You're only seeing what's there. You hit a strike."

He stood and she went to the bench and let her knees collapse beneath her. She wasn't sure which was harder to believe. That he thought she was the prettiest girl in the place or that she'd managed to hit that strike. Not that it was her first strike of the night, it wasn't. But how had she done it when she could barely focus?

After four games, dinner and more laughing than Ava could remember doing in a long time, they called it a night. She was a little nervous about getting back on the motorcycle but not as bad as before the ride over here.

"Do you need help getting it on or you want me to let you try?" Cowboy asked, handing her a helmet.

"Let me try. If I can't figure it out, I'll ask."

"All right." He reached for his own and had it on and fastened before she finally gave up. She just couldn't manage to get the two ends of the clip lined up to fit together.

"I give up." Ava tilted her head back, trying to give him as much room as he might need to get the clip together.

"No problem." His voice was muffled through the heavy helmet. He took the two ends and fitted them together in seconds. She didn't know what he did but the next thing she knew, his voice was crystal clear and as if he was right there in the helmet with her.

"You want to go straight home or ride around a little first?"

Ava tilted her head to one side, thinking. "Let's ride a bit." She didn't say it but thought she wouldn't panic this time when she didn't know where they were.

This time he didn't have to tell her where to put her feet or re-position her legs once she was on, that made her feel at least a little less incompetent.

"Ready?" He turned his head back, as if he were trying to look at her, though she couldn't see how he could see her with the helmet on.

"Ready." She wrapped her arms around him and waited while he once more walked the bike backward, then they zoomed forward. Or at least it felt like that to Ava. They were still in the parking lot and probably doing under ten miles an hour, it just seemed fast to her.

B y the time they made it back to her apartment, Ava had relaxed and wasn't holding onto Cowboy quite so tight, at least in her opinion. She could see why people thought riding a motorcycle was fun. It wasn't something she wanted to do every day, she liked her car, but she could get into it, especially with Cowboy.

He pulled the bike into the same space he'd been in when he picked her up. She got off the bike then watched as he did the same, while she tried to figure out how to release the catch on the helmet. Cowboy took off his helmet and hung it on the handlebars, then turned to watch her. Ava appreciated that he didn't try to take over but let her struggle until she was ready for his help. When she gave up in frustration and let her hands drop with a sigh, he didn't make her ask, just reached up with one hand and popped the latch. He didn't lift it off for her but let her do that at her own pace.

"I don't know how you can get this thing off and on so easily." She handed him the helmet.

"Practice." He shot her a grin before hanging her helmet on the other end of the handlebars. "I fasten them several times a day. It's almost second nature to me." He walked her toward the building and took her right to her door.

"Why don't you come in for a while?" She wasn't ready for this night to end. She liked him and she wanted more but wasn't sure how to ask for it.

"I'd like to, but I'm afraid more would happen than you're ready for."

Ava couldn't help the frown that creased her brow as she stood beside him in front of her door.

"What do you mean?"

"That's exactly what I mean. You are sweet and mostly innocent. I like you, more than a little. And I want to do this again, but you're not ready for what you think you want. I'm not going to just drop you here though."

"Then what are you going to do?" She was even more confused. What did he mean she was innocent? She'd been married for nearly fifteen years. How could she be innocent anymore?

"I've been wanting to do this all night, but in the middle of the bowling alley wasn't the right place, even if it wasn't busy." He slowly lowered his face to hers.

Ava saw him coming and thought there was time to stop him, but why? If he wouldn't come inside, at least she would get a kiss. Man did she want that kiss. She ached to know what he tasted like, what his hands felt like on her body. She wasn't going to get everything she wanted, but she'd take what she could get.

Cowboy's mouth covered hers and she didn't hesitate to open her lips beneath his probing tongue. Her hands found their way to his arms, as if of their own accord. She lost herself in the feel of his arms as they went around her. His kiss turned hot, searing every thought from her mind but him.

More.

She needed more. Her fingers curled into his arms as she tried to pull him closer. A soft sound escaped from her throat as he pulled away.

"Damn, angel. You taste as sweet as you look."

Ava stared up at him, dazed. "Come inside."

Cowboy shook his head. "Angel, you're tempting as hell but not tonight. You're not the kind of woman to take a man to bed on the first date. Even I know that. I'll call tomorrow and see if you want to do something soon. Give you a little time to make sure this dirty old biker is what you really want." He dropped a brief soft kiss on her lips before releasing her and taking a step back. "Be warned though, I don't know if I'll be able to do the right thing and walk away a second time." He motioned to the door. "Inside before I leave. I want to make sure you're safe before I go."

She did as he instructed, unlocked the door, and stepped inside, turning to watch him as the door closed. She wished he'd stayed but somehow because he'd refused, she wanted him even more.

# 9

Cowboy stowed the extra helmet, got on his bike, and went back to the clubhouse, ignoring the snug fit of his jeans. Fuck that woman was hot. He wished he could have stayed, but she was an angel. Not the kind of woman who slept around like he had for the last ten plus years. She needed wooing. And damned if he didn't want to be the one to give it to her.

In the parking lot, he sat on the bike for a minute, trying to force his body to behave. He thought about something else, anything else but Ava. The club, the difficulties he'd had with it in the last six months. The trouble Rooster and Jonesy had been causing over the last couple months.

Unlike Tank, they hadn't had records and had gotten out on bail while they waited for their trials to begin for the abduction and assault on a man who'd come to town trying to figure out who was harassing his club.

All that had gone down months ago, and Tank, who had been the Kings of Destruction president at the time, had been using the club for his personal business without the knowledge or consent of the rest of the club. That alone had gotten him stripped of his patch when he'd been caught and arrested for the crime, along with the flunkies who had been in on it and known what he was doing, Rooster and Jonesy.

Tank was still in jail. His previous prison time, and the ties he'd made there that facilitated this criminal activity had ensured the judge denied bail. He was the least of the Kings problems, unless he was still pulling strings. Cowboy wouldn't put that past him. But how could he prove it? As far as he had been able to figure out, he couldn't.

He realized he was still sitting on his bike, stepped off and went inside. There he found Deacon, his best friend, and the man he'd tapped as VP when he had become president.

"Where you been?" Deke asked as Cowboy pulled out a chair at his brother's table and sat.

"Out."

Deke lifted a single brow at him, then turned and waved at the prospect behind the bar, motioning for him to bring them a round, then turned his attention back to Cowboy. "Out, huh? This have anything to do with that hot piece of ass you had your eye on the other night?"

Fury rose in Cowboy, but he did his best to tamp it down. Deke was only using the same terms Cowboy had used himself for years. He had no way of knowing that Ava was different and to jump to her defense would tip his friend off that something was different.

Cowboy wasn't quite ready to do that. Not yet. After Ava decided if she wanted to see him again. If she was willing to go for a rough biker rather than her usual strait-laced man of God type. Cowboy shook his head at the way his thoughts had turned.

"You have a one-track mind, you know that?" Cowboy said. "Any new trouble?"

Deke shook his head. "They've been quiet. Almost too quiet. I feel like they're getting ready to pull something and I just don't know what."

"Me either. Have the rest of the brothers keep an eye out for them. Don't go hunting them down, but keep your eyes peeled. They'll turn up again. Especially since they blame us." Cowboy shook his head and wished things could have been different.

If Tank had come to the club with what he'd wanted to do. If the other men hadn't gone along, even though they knew it was without the club's permission. If, if, if. There were a million of them. Hell, if Tank had brought the job to the club, they probably would have approved it. It was that he involved the club in criminal acts without their permission. You don't do things like that, not to your brothers. At least not more than once.

Stripping them of their patches had been the right move, Cowboy had no doubt. He just wished he wasn't the one who had to deal with the fall out. While the vote to strip them hadn't been unanimous, it had been overwhelmingly in favor and most of the few who'd voted against it had remained. They didn't seem unhappy in the club, just not thrilled that the members they were closest to were no longer here.

"What are you doing tonight?" Cowboy turned his attention to Deke.

"Not much. Sitting here watching the comings and goings. Listening to what's being said." Deke tipped up his bottle and took a long pull then set it back down on the table. "Just trying to stay on top of what's going on with the brothers. The last thing we need is a mutiny – after last winter; that might be the death of the Kings.

"We need something to build us up. Both as a brotherhood and as a family. Where's Miles?" Cowboy looked around until he spotted the man he was looking for. "MILES!"

When the other man looked his way, Cowboy waved him over. When the other man reached them, Cowboy kicked a chair out from the table.

"Have a seat. We need to talk."

Miles looked from Cowboy to Deacon and back again for a moment then pulled out the chair and sat.

"What can I do for you?"

"I need you to do some planning for me. We need events," Cowboy said.

"You can enlist help if you need it. We have several things we want done over the next few months," Deke said.

"I want at least two rides and one family event," Cowboy glanced at Deke.

"Per month," Deke put in. "Every month until at least October. Between now and then we'll decide what we want over the winter."

"There can be more, but that's the minimum. I want one family event a month in town. There can be additional, either here or family runs. The two minimum runs are to be brothers only, but again, there can be more. Questions?" Cowboy turned to Miles.

"Do we have a mileage minimum for any of the runs? Destinations? What is the point, other than to ride?"

"Not sure on milage yet, let's start with no minimum. But we'll look at getting a milage goal set up soon. We can also do some destination runs. That would be fun for the family events too. And the point is brotherhood. We have relationships to rebuild, and this is how we do it."

"All right. I can do this. How soon do you want the first event?"

"Soon. Next week if you can pull it off. You can start with a brothers only run to give yourself time to plan something bigger."

Miles nodded slowly, as if he was already deep in thought.

"Holidays make obvious times for local family events. Memorial Day is only a couple of weeks away. I'd better get started on that too." He blinked and gave his head a shake then turned back to Cowboy. "You said I could enlist help. Any limits on that?"

Cowboy shook his head. "If they're not busy with other club business, you're welcome to them."

"Good. I'm going to need a lot of it over the next couple weeks. A run for next weekend, and a BBQ for the one after that." He started to stand then sat back down and looked at Cowboy. "Was that all?"

"Do you want more?"

"Not really but I was making sure I wasn't leaving before you were done."

"That's all, for now."

Miles gave him a curt nod, then stood and hurried off to get started on all the details, Cowboy was sure.

"Making the event's monthly was a good call. I hadn't thought that far ahead."

"That's part of being president. You also might start thinking about those winter events. Rides will be dangerous, but we can do other things. I think that's part of where Tank screwed up, aside from the obvious, of course."

Cowboy fell silent for a few minutes as he considered different options. He needed to get details from Miles about this weekend, then have a meeting with all the brothers to explain what he was doing and how it would benefit the Kings. And he needed to make time to see Ava again. If she was up for it.

He tipped back his bottle and drained it.

"I'm calling it a night. You know how to reach me." He left the bottle on the table next to Deke. The prospect would clean it up later and went to the door. He wanted to sleep in his own bed tonight.

※※※※ ※※※※

At home in his apartment, Cowboy turned on the TV, took off his boots and sat back in the recliner. He stared at the screen while flipping through channels until he got bored with not being able to find anything to catch his interest and went to bed. He was asleep nearly as soon as his head hit the pillow.

When he woke, he lay in bed and stretched before getting up and shuffling into the bathroom for a hot shower. As was his habit, he stepped into the tub, then turned on the water, letting that first blast of cold water hit him in the face. He'd found that first few seconds of cold water did more to wake him than a whole pot of coffee. Not that he passed on the coffee, it just wasn't what woke him in the morning.

When the water warmed, Cowboy turned so it sprayed down his neck and back. The strong spray and the heat of the water beat the stiffness from his muscles left by several hours of laying stationary. While he let the water do its magic, he let his mind drift back to Ava.

He couldn't help but wonder if it was her habit to shower in the mornings before work? One thought led to another and before he knew what he what he was doing, Cowboy was picturing her naked and wet in the shower. It didn't take much imagination for him to picture her there in his shower with him.

He shouldn't be doing this, he knew, but what would it harm? He took a palm full of soap and lathered up. He let the water beat down on his back, closed his eyes and pictured Ava there in the shower with him.

How she would blush, he had no doubt. But she was up for just about anything and he was sure she'd be game to shower, and more, with him, if he asked her. He pictured her pretty blush, the way it would cover her entire body. He imagined the pretty pink covering her tits. Tits he was sure would fill his palm and more. He ran his lathered hand down his belly and lower, cupping his balls for a moment as he imagined his hand was Ava's. The delicate fingers running over his skin, cupping his balls, and sliding up the length of his rod.

Cowboy let his hand follow the path he imagined hers would take, then her mouth. He couldn't help but imagine the sweet pressure of her tongue running along his length as he wrapped his own hand around is cock, and slide it along the length to the tip, then back down to the base.

He groaned as he repeated the motion, losing himself in the sensations that paired with the images in his head, sent fire racing along his spine. It didn't take long until a curse ripped itself from his lips as he exploded all over his hand and the shower wall.

With a sigh, he cleaned himself up, finished his shower and dressed for the day.

# 10

As Ava prepared for work the next morning, she considered what Cowboy had said the night before. Did she really want to get involved with a biker?

He was nothing like Hank. That was a point in his favor, not one against him. If she had her way, she'd never get mixed up with a man like Hank again. She also wasn't fool enough to swear off men all together. There had been parts of marriage she'd liked, though, even that hadn't met with Hank's approval. He'd told her it was unseemly for the wife of a pastor to be interested or as receptive to that part of marriage. At least that was what he'd told her. He hadn't seemed to mind that Andrea had liked it. At least from what she'd seen when she'd walked in on them.

Ava pushed thoughts of Hank and Andrea out of her mind. He wasn't in charge of her anymore, and she wasn't going to let his likes or dislikes rule her life anymore.

What she needed to do was figure out what she wanted. But since Cowboy was the first person ever to ask, she hadn't given it much thought.

What did she want? Ava asked herself as she applied her makeup and styled her hair. The obvious answer was that she wanted to live. But that sounded silly and simplistic, even to herself. She needed something more definite, something with more substance.

A list. She needed to make a list. That would help her figure it out. She took a legal pad from her desk and took it in the kitchen when she went to refill her coffee and get something to eat before she had to leave for work.

While she ate her bowl of oatmeal, she ran a line of numbers down the side of the page. Now came the hard part. Now she had to decide what she wanted.

1. Make my own decisions, good or bad.

2. Experience life – all of it, not just what other people think she should.

3. Someone to love her who cares what she wants.

4. Someone to share her life and experiences with that she can love.

5.

She stared at the paper for several minutes, unable to come up with anything else. Even tapping her pen against the pad brought no new thoughts, until she noticed the time. She hurried to wash her breakfast dishes and get out the door.

If she didn't hurry, she'd be late.

She made it out the door just in time. As she started her car, she couldn't help but wonder where Cowboy was and what he was doing.

Would he call her tonight? She hoped so. It wasn't until she was headed into the bank that it occurred to her that she had his number. She didn't need to wait for him to call her. She could call him if she wanted.

By the time Ava's shift ended and she walked out at the end of the day, her feet throbbed and her back ached.

She looked forward to a nice soak in a tub of hot water. Wait. Didn't her apartment complex have a hot tub? She thought she remembered seeing one the last time she'd gone to the office. Maybe it was time to dig out her swim suit and find out. Where had she put them? When she'd been in Arizona, she'd owned several, but had she kept any?

She had been so determined for a fresh start. She did recall thinking why would she need a swimsuit way up here in North Dakota, where it was cold. After all, it would never be as hot here as it got in Arizona. She wondered again, had she brought a swimsuit with her? The more she thought about it, the more she was certain swimsuits were among the many things she had left behind.

Well, that was one thing out, at least for tonight. Most likely. She would make sure there was a hot tub, then go get herself a new suit, this time without having to worry about if it was proper for the wife of a pastor to be seen in.

That thought put a smile on her face.

It gave her another thing to add to her list.

1. Wear clothes that she liked without worrying about what others think.

At home, she went inside, kicked off her shoes and went into the bedroom where she made a cursory search of her drawers for a swimsuit there. When she didn't find one easily, she gave up. It just meant she needed a shopping trip.

She wasn't going today, but that didn't mean she couldn't get an idea of what she wanted. She took her laptop, a gift from Aaron when she'd arrived in Dickenson. She'd never been allowed to have a computer of her own before she'd left Hank. Though she did have a smart phone, Hank had insisted there wasn't the money for more than one computer and since he was the one who earned the money, the computer had been his. Again, she pushed thoughts of Hank from her mind as she carried her computer to her recliner and put her feet up while she pulled up the website to her favorite clothing store.

Ava didn't know how long she spent looking at clothes and swimsuits but when she found herself yawning, she realized she'd lost track of time. It was nearly bedtime, and she'd forgotten to have dinner. After thinking a moment, she decided she wasn't hungry, but she did want that hot soak, so she went for the bathroom to run the water. While the tub filled, she went for her phone, where she'd left it to charge in the kitchen.

She'd missed three messages. Two from Aaron, and one from Cowboy. She skipped the texts from her brother, he was likely just checking on her, and went straight to the one from Cowboy.

**Cowboy:** *Hope you had a good day. Have you given up the idea of an old biker yet?*

Ava shook her head as she typed out a reply.

**Ava:** *Not at all. I had a long day and I'm about to go to bed. But I've been thinking of you.*

She hit send and carried her phone into the bathroom with her in case he replied. Then stripped and stepped into the tub of hot water, sighing as she relaxed and let the heat soak away the soreness from her day.

# 11

Cowboy walked into the clubhouse, still dirty and grimy from a day in the shop. But he'd gotten a lot done, so felt good about it. He stopped inside the door and scanned the room. It only took him a moment to spot the man he was looking for sitting at a table in the corner, several notebooks scattered on the table in front of him. Cowboy motioned to the prospect behind the bar to bring them a couple drinks, then he headed for Miles.

"Make any progress?" Cowboy pulled out a chair and sat.

"Yeah. Some." Miles barely looked up from his notes.

"Talk to me about it."

"Ride this weekend. Destination ride. We go to the Devil's Tower. Leave early, stay a couple hours, come back. It's a long day, but it will build bonds. That's what we're after, right?"

"It is. Anything still need to be done for this weekend?"

"Just someone to pack the food we're going to need to take. There's no place to get food at the Tower and I don't want to have to worry about having to find someplace big enough for all of us. What I'm debating right now is cold food or having the prospects bring a truck and tow the grill."

Cowboy thought about it for a minute, then said, "Take the trailer. Let's make it an event. The truck means we can fill it with ice chests full of food, lots of water, some pop, but no booze. Not even beer. We can get into that when we get home and won't be on the roads."

"Got it." Miles took a few notes in the notebook to his right, then looked back up at Cowboy. "Any other preference on the menu?"

"Keep it simple, real food. Burgers, brats, something like that."

Miles took a few more notes then pushed that notebook away and pulled another in front of him. "Now let's talk about the next weekend. The holiday BBQ. I'm thinking the club supplies the meat, everyone brings some kind of side dish, dessert, or drink. Again, keep it casual, and having each family bring a dish guarantees there will be something there they like. Doing it potluck style also gives people something to talk about. Did you like this, no, how was that, how did you make this, can I get the recipe for that? That kind of thing."

"Sounds like you've got things well in hand. Do you need anything else from me?"

Miles scanned the table and the notebooks scattered there. "I think I have things handled. Oh. Budgets. For both of this month's events and the others going forward."

"Talk to Caden. See what we can afford and if we need to do something to raise money for this." Cowboy hadn't liked putting someone so much younger in charge of the club's money, but Caden was a wiz when it came to making money multiply.

"Will do. If something else comes up, can I reach out?"

"Of course. I want to be approachable to all of the brothers. But you're working on something for me, so, of course, you can reach out. I'm calling a meeting tomorrow night and unveiling this. I've got a few things I want us to vote on. These runs are among them. So be prepared to answer questions on them."

Miles frowned for a moment, then blinked and shrugged. "Okay, I can do that."

"Ideally, you'll also have at least a basic plan for each month for the rest of the summer, but I know it's short notice and you may not have time for that."

"Thanks for the heads up. I'll see what I can put together." Miles pulled yet another notebook in front of him, opened it and took more notes. The front door squeaked open, drawing Cowboy's attention. He turned in time to see Deke step inside.

"If you need anything from me, let me know. Otherwise, I'll leave you to your planning."

Miles lifted one hand in a wave, but didn't reply as Cowboy stood, moved to a new table, and waved Deke over. As Deke made his way to him, Cowboy signaled the prospect for another round.

"Have a seat." Cowboy motioned to the chair beside him when Deke reached him.

Deke glanced toward the bar, then pulled out a chair and sat. "What's up tonight?"

"Club business. I need you to call a meeting for tomorrow night. It's short notice but I want to give them more notice for Saturday."

"What's Saturday?"

"The first of the summer runs. I've got some things I want to put to the club for voting tomorrow. We need as many present as possible."

"Okay, I'll call the meeting. Do I get to know what's up or is it going to be sprung on me like it is on them?"

Cowboy stayed quiet while the prospect brought their beer. Once the kid, who was probably 20 or 21 now that he thought about it, left, he focused on Deke again.

"We're going to vote on runs, milage, mandatory runs, that kind of thing."

Deke frowned.

Cowboy sighed, took a pull from his drink, and started over. "You heard what I told Miles last night. I want to propose that it be mandatory to make at least one brothers only event each month. Either one is acceptable, or both if they want, but they need to make at least one. Family events will be harder. I want some kind of contribution from each brother, but I understand that not all the families have anything to do with the club, so I won't make attendance mandatory. But they will be heavily encouraged."

Deke was quiet a moment. "We're putting on three events a month and only one will be mandatory?"

"Three to four. I've got Miles looking to doing family trips too. We could potentially have events every weekend all summer long."

"That could be good and bad. I think overall it will be good, giving the brothers somewhere to go, something to do and less chance to decide they're bored and stir shit they shouldn't be involved in."

"That was kind of my thought. I do have something I need you to do if you don't mind."

"What?"

"Reach out to that club we had trouble with last winter. The Demented Souls. Reach out to Ghost or Malice and let them know we're going to be in their neck of the woods this weekend."

"We're going to Wyoming?"

Cowboy nodded as he took another drink of his beer. "This weekend's run is down to the Devil's Tower. We'll have the prospects bring a truck and the grill, make a day of it. Just let the Souls know we'll be in their area, but it's a day trip and we're not stirring trouble. We're just giving them a head's up, so they don't think we're moving in on them."

"I can do that. Any other messages for me to deliver while I'm playing messenger?"

"Not that I can think of, but I'll let you know. You learn anything else after I left last night?"

"Nothing of any consequence. There was some belly aching, but nothing serious. I think you've hit on something with this plan. Events every weekend will build a bond between the Kings again." Deke shook his head. "I know Tank won the last election. Hell, I even voted for him, same as you. But the farther we get from his rule, the more I can see it was a mistake. It wasn't the best interests of the Kings he had in mind, though he talked a good game. If we could do things over, we could avoid the crap he got us into."

"And if wishes were horses, everyone would ride," Cowboy said. "No point in bemoaning our mistakes, and a lot of us made that one. What matters now is how we learn from it and what we do moving forward. And right now, the priority is calling that meeting. You can reach out to the Souls whenever you're ready, as long as they know by Friday that we're coming down Saturday."

"Got it. What time tomorrow for the meeting?"

Cowboy thought about it for a moment. Too early would mean taking time from kids and families, but too late would mean stealing sleep from his brothers. He didn't want to do either if he could help it.

"Nine. This shouldn't take more than an hour, then they can get on with whatever they need to do."

"Ten-four."

# 12

By the time Ava walked out of the bank Tuesday evening, she'd made up her mind. She had no intention of walking away from Cowboy. Even if he did keep calling himself a 'dirty biker.' She hated that phrase.

Had he meant that he had a dirty job? She couldn't imagine that designing and building custom bikes was any cleaner than being a mechanic. Not that she cared. He worked, who cared what the job was? Had he meant something else? She didn't know but she wasn't going to ask because she hated that phrase and the next time he used it she would tell him so.

Now she had to gather the nerve to call Cowboy and tell him what she'd decided. But not just yet. Now she was going to dinner with Belinda. Aaron had been called out of town this morning and when Belinda had called asking Ava out, she'd jumped at the chance to get to know her sister-in-law better.

No small part of it was that she was looking forward to a girls' night. She couldn't remember the last time she'd had girlfriends to go hang out with.

In her car, she started the engine, and turned on the AC, then pulled out her phone to check for any messages from Belinda before heading home to change. There was nothing from Belinda, but there was one from Cowboy.

**Cowboy:** *What are your plans for tonight?*

Ava didn't see any reason not to tell him.

**Ava:** *Dinner with my sister-in-law. Aaron had to go out of town.*

She finished typing her message and hit send, then set her phone aside and put the car in gear. She needed to get home and change if she was going to meet Belinda on time.

After she'd gotten ready for dinner, she checked her messages again. This time there was one from Belinda, but she skipped it to read the one from Cowboy first

**Cowboy:** *Have fun.*

Disappointment zinged through her. She didn't know what she'd hoped for, but it was more than that. Checking the message from Belinda, she found the name and address of the restaurant they would be meeting at for dinner.

Ava didn't yet know how to respond to Cowboy, so she didn't. Instead, she sent a message to Belinda letting her know she would be there soon, squared her shoulders and left for the restaurant.

***

"Tell me about your date. Who was it with, how did it go?" Belinda's eyes lit with excitement and curiosity as she turned to Ava. They'd already placed their orders, now had nothing to do but wait, and chat.

Ava's face heated. She'd suspected Belinda would be asking but she hadn't been expecting this much excitement or interest.

"It was good." She didn't know what else to say.

"Who is he? Where did you go? What did you do? Did you get laid?"

Ava's face flamed. "His name is Cowboy. We had talked about a movie, but there was nothing interesting playing locally, so he asked if I wanted to go to Billings or find something else to do… I suggested we go bowling."

"Bowling?" Belinda crinkled her nose.

"You should try it sometime. It's more fun than you'd think. You don't have to keep a running conversation because you take turns. And you get to see what kind of sport he is. How he plays and how he takes not being the best at everything, unless he bowls all the time. Because without regular practice, no one bowls well."

"Valid points and smart too. Plus, it's public and well lit, in case they turn out to be a creep."

"Exactly."

"Well, how did bowling go?"

"Really well. I had a lot of fun and I'm sure he did too."

"Fun. I'm still stuck on fun bowling." Belinda laughed.

"Have you ever been bowling?"

"No. It's such an old folk sport."

Ava smiled. Belinda wasn't the first person she'd met to say so. She'd said something similar way back when they'd gone bowling in school, but she'd soon learned otherwise.

"Don't knock it till you try it."

"So where did you end up eating?"

"At the bowling alley. The food is pretty good. And we were having fun so why stop and go somewhere else?"

"You could always have taken him home. And don't say you did, because if you had, you wouldn't be that bright shade of scarlet. By the way, what kind of name is Cowboy?"

"A nickname. And I tried to take him home or rather I invited him in after he took me home, but he said no. He said," she fell quiet a moment as she tried to remember exactly what Cowboy had said to her, "he said I wasn't ready for what I thought I wanted, and he wanted to give me time to be sure. Then he planted what I think might be the hottest kiss I've ever experienced on me."

Belinda blinked a couple times. "Not ready for what you think you wanted? What did he mean by that?"

Ava pulled her mouth to one side. "We'd done a lot of talking and getting to know each other. As much as I try not to talk about Hank, as we're talking small bits come out."

"Like?"

"Like that I was married young, only recently divorced, a very brief bit about how I ended up divorced."

"Oh god. You didn't tell him that bit about slipping her the holy ghost did you?" Belinda's face turned red as she looked at Ava horrified at the idea.

"No," Ava laughed, "but he would find it as funny as I do. Anyway, he's kind of protective. He wants to make sure I'm not rushing into anything I'll regret later or something really reckless that could get me hurt. He said he wanted me to be sure that a dirty old biker was what I really wanted." Ava shook her head. "I get where he's coming from. A lot of people get out of a restrictive relationship and go wild." She wasn't about to admit how she'd met Cowboy, and that she was one of those people who'd gone wild, or done something really stupid.

"That is sweet, as long as you're sure he's not going to be just as controlling and domineering as Hank was. You just got out of that situation. You don't want to get into another one just like it."

"I'm sure. He's doing something I don't think I remember Hank doing ever. Not even when we were first married or even dating. He asks what I want." They paused as the waitress brought their food, noticed they needed new drinks, and disappeared.

"That's good. As long as it's not just an act to reel you in, then he'll turn into that domineering kind of guy."

"I guess it's possible, but I really don't think so. He doesn't seem like that kind of guy."

"Your date was two days ago, when he refused to come into your place with you. Have you heard from him since?"

"Yeah. We've been texting every day."

Belinda's brows shot up. "Every day?" The waitress came back with new drinks for each of them, then left them to eat.

Ava nodded. "Every day. Not long, drawn out conversations but checking on me, asking what my plans are for the evening."

They ate in silence for a moment, each lost in their own thoughts. After a while Belinda spoke again.

"Wait, you said biker. Have you ever even been on a motorcycle?"

"Yes, as a matter of fact, I have." Ava gave her sister-in-law a superior look, though she knew she wouldn't be able to keep a straight face for long.

Belinda's eyes went wide. "You have? When?"

"Cowboy took me for a ride when we went out the other night." She couldn't help but grin at the look of shock on Belinda's face.

"You got on the back of a bike with a stranger. Did you even know anything about him?"

"I knew he was a good guy."

"How?"

Ava shrugged. "I just knew." She wasn't telling Belinda about her night at the bar. Her sister-in-law would tell Aaron then Ava would never hear the end of it. "We had a good time, and we've been talking. I'm sure we'll be seeing each other again soon."

"How much of him do you plan on seeing?"

Ava bit her lip, then looked up and met Belinda's gaze. "All of him, if I can talk him into it." She couldn't help the laugh that burst free. "But seriously. I like him. A lot. If he wants a fling, I'll take it. If he's willing to go for more, I'm willing to see how far things go."

"But he's so different from Hank."

"That's exactly my point. I'm not looking for another great love to last the rest of my life. I'm looking to live life. To experience it, not just watch it go by. Even if that means a series of shorter relationships. If Cowboy can do that with me for a while, I'll take it. If he's not interested, someone else will be, or I can do it on my own for a while. I've learned that while someone to share life with is great, it's not necessary. I can have a lot of fun on my own," Ava said with a shrug.

She hoped she sounded more nonchalant than she felt about it. She liked Cowboy a lot. She didn't want to think about how badly it would hurt if he walked away.

# 13

C owboy found his mind drifting, and not for the first time today. He shook his head, trying to shake loose thoughts of a certain blonde, then bent his head back to the sketch he was trying to finish. The client had called this morning with some changes he wanted made, and now Cowboy was trying to make his ideas work on the bike they'd been back and forth on for the last three months.

He was hopeful this last design would be approved. Then the client would send the next payment installment and they could start fabrication. That was the part Cowboy really loved. The designing was good, but the building was where his heart lay.

The goal was to finish this sketch and send it off to the client today, so it could be approved or reworked yet again. And the sooner he finished the sketch, the sooner he could go help with the finishing touches on the last bike he was working on. It would be ready for its new owner within the week, so he wanted to make sure everything was just right.

A few more pencil strokes and he leaned back to take a look at it. That was perfect. He scanned the images and emailed them to the client then lifted his arms over his head and arched his back as he stretched. Ava slipped into his mind again, he couldn't help but wonder what she would think of some of the bikes he'd designed. Would she like a ride on one?

He needed to check in with her. The new bike would need a test drive. Maybe she'd like to go along with him? Cowboy rolled his eyes and shook his head at how flighty he'd become over this woman. Still, he reached for his phone and typed out a quick message.

**Cowboy:** *How's your day been?*

He stared at the screen for several seconds as if her reply would appear instantly on his screen then realized he was being stupid. He stood, shoved his phone in his pocket and headed out to the shop.

The noise in the shop was loud but familiar. He checked on what each man was doing, making sure things were turning out the way they should before he went to the bike that had just finished painting and needed to be assembled. He ran one hand along the gas tank, making sure the finish was smooth, then got to work fitting pieces into the frame, assembling the bike. Of all the construction, this was one part he insisted on doing himself. The final assembly, making sure everything was just right before they delivered the product.

He didn't know how long he'd been working when Deke walked in.

"What are you doing still here?"

"Working, obviously," Cowboy bit back the urge to snarl as he replied. Why did people have to ask such stupid questions when the answer was obvious?

"I was surprised you weren't at the clubhouse. We've got a meeting in fifteen minutes. A meeting you called, if you'll recall."

Cowboy looked up from where he was fitting one particularly difficult piece into place. "Shit. Is it really that late?"

Deke didn't dignify that with a response, just looked at him as if to say, would I be here if it weren't?

Cowboy stood, grabbed a rag, and started scrubbing at his hands. He was in the final stages, so they weren't too dirty, still, he needed to get washed up and go. He glanced down at his overalls and shrugged. They'd have to do. He didn't have time to change right now.

Cowboy leaned back in his chair, tipped back his drink, and drained the last few swallows. The meeting had gone better than he'd hoped. Not only had all his proposals passed, but the men had been enthusiastic at his ideas, even when he'd said he wanted it mandatory that everyone make at least one of the brothers only events each month.

He pulled his phone out and turned it back on, as he'd shut it off for the meeting. As it powered up and found signal, it buzzed with several incoming messages. The only ones he cared about right now were the ones from Ava.

**Ava:** *Day was good. Work was boring but busy and went by fast. I'm exhausted and headed to bed.*

**Ava:** *Want to do something this weekend?*

He stared at the screen and cursed that he had to be on the ride this weekend. He was looking forward to the ride and since he'd ordered it organized, and had it made mandatory to make at least one ride a month, he couldn't really say sorry, I'd rather spend the time with my girl. Especially not for the first event.

With a sigh, he typed up a reply.

**Cowboy:** *I'd love to. I'm busy Saturday, but I can do Friday night or any time on Sunday. When are you free?*

He hit send then checked the time. Ten-thirty. She was probably fast asleep. He should probably head home and go to bed himself. Cowboy couldn't help but feel accomplished as he stood.

"Headed home?" Deke asked.

"I am. I want to finish that assembly tomorrow. You going to come by?"

"I may. I'll let you know."

"All right. Have a good night." Cowboy tipped one hand in a wave.

"You too." Deke watched him go.

Cowboy walked across the parking lot to where he'd parked his bike in front of the shop, stepped astride it and headed home, his thoughts not on the bike he needed to finish assembling, but instead on Ava and what they might do this weekend.

He didn't know if she was ready to go all the way to Billings on the bike, but he could take her in his truck, if she wanted to see a movie. On the other hand, bowling had been fun. What other things like that could he suggest? Things that weren't common date things but could be fun. He was halfway home when he wondered if she might enjoy going to the batting cages. It wasn't bowling, but it could be fun. He didn't think there was a laser tag place in town, but he'd investigate it. Then he'd give her some options, see what she was interested in.

He liked that she opted for less traditional dates. It was fun and kept him wondering what she would pick next. Maybe he should investigate some more offbeat options. He'd love to find an option she hadn't thought of.

Cowboy pulled into the parking lot at his complex, parked and went up to his apartment. He needed to research what kind of activities they had locally. It had been too long since he'd looked for anything new to do.

# 14

The talk with Belinda was still on her mind when Ava had gotten into bed the night before. She had thought about her determination to experience things and not just get through life, whether there was someone there to share the experiences with her or not. She had wondered what she would do this weekend if Cowboy wasn't available? She let the thought linger in the back of her mind as she'd laid there wishing he'd text her back.

Frustrated that he hadn't answered her, she'd pulled out her laptop and looked up things to do around Dickenson. She woke the next morning feeling good that she had a plan for the weekend, well for Saturday anyway. She had a couple of ideas for Sunday if she didn't hear from Cowboy.

She finished her morning routine, dressed, and made it into the kitchen for coffee. While the coffee brewed, she picked up her phone. There was a message from Cowboy. A glance at when he'd sent it told her it had been well after she'd gone to bed the night before.

The message said he was busy Saturday but up for something Friday or Sunday. As well as a second message sent this morning.

**Cowboy:** *Want to do something for dinner tonight?*

She stared at the screen wondering how to reply. Yes, she was up for dinner, but she didn't want to seem to eager. Then again. It had been hours since he'd sent the message. She typed up a response telling him she was open, asking if they would be on the bike and what time to be ready then hit send. By the time she'd finished that, her coffee was ready. She stood for a moment after the first couple of sips, letting the rich flavor do as much to wake her up as the hit of caffeine would once it hit her bloodstream. After a moment she took her cup and headed for the bedroom to finish getting ready for work.

***

**B**elinda: *So, when you going to see your hottie again?*

Ava rolled her eyes and shook her head as she set the phone aside to start the car. She wanted to get the air conditioner started before responding to her sister-in-law. Once she was comfortable, the door closed and air blowing, she picked up the phone and typed out her response.

**Ava:** *Dinner tonight.*

She'd wondered all day long if Cowboy had gotten back to her and what he'd said, but she wasn't allowed to have her phone with her at the window. She understood why. It was a security risk since she handled people's account information all day long. Not that she would do anything with it, but there were many not as scrupulous as she was.

She'd checked at lunch, but there hadn't been a reply yet. On her way out to the car, Belinda's message had been the first to pop up. Now she navigated to his message.

**Cowboy:** *How's seven? And I'd love to take the bike if you're up for it.*

Did she want to go out on the bike tonight? She had this morning, but now her feet ached.

No, she reminded herself, she was going to live life, not watch it pass her by.

**Ava:** *The bike would be great, and I'll be ready by seven.*

She dropped her phone back into her purse and turned her attention to the wheel. If she was going to be ready, she needed to get home.

By the time she pulled into her space at the complex, she'd mentally moved past her reluctance to change and get ready and was excited to see Cowboy again. She wondered if he had something in mind or would he ask her what she wanted to do. Not that it mattered. After researching the area last night, she had a list of things she wanted to do and places she wanted to try. If he asked, she'd mention one of those. In the meantime, she needed to get changed.

Inside her apartment she hung up her purse and headed for the bedroom, stripping out of the semi-dressy clothes she wore for work. She'd long since gotten used to dresses and skirts, as that was what Hank expected her to wear all the time. Jeans were not considered appropriate unless they were doing something rough or grubby like moving or yard work.

Now, she loved the freedom of wearing what she wanted and what her mood called for and she loved that Cowboy encouraged that. She shucked her skirt and hose, then pulled her favorite pair of jeans from the closet and stepped into them. She grabbed her favorite pair of cowboy boots from the corner where she kept them and set them in front of the chair so she could put them on in a minute before turning back to the closet and trying to decide what top to wear.

She stood staring at the closet for a long time. Not that the selection was huge or much varied once you removed her work clothes from the options. But there was that halter top she'd bought on a whim and had never had the nerve to wear.

Should she?

Would Cowboy think she was too old to wear something that fun and girlish? As those thoughts flitted across her mind, they solidified her decision. She would wear it and to hell with what he thought.

She pulled the bright red halter from the hanger and put it on, taking in her reflection and having second thoughts before she firmly pushed those doubts from her mind and went to fix her hair. She'd pulled it back high on her head this morning, and that wouldn't work if they were taking the motorcycle tonight.

She'd just stepped into her boots, stood, and checked her appearance in the mirror when a knock sounded on her door. She wondered who it could be, but a glance at the clock told her it was five minutes to seven and probably Cowboy. She grabbed her jacket and went to answer it.

She tossed the strap to her purse over her head and stuffed one arm into the sleeve of her jacket as she opened the door.

"I'm ready," she said in greeting as she tried to find the other arm of the jacket.

"Did you even check to see who was at the door before opening it?" Cowboy scowled at her.

Ava bit the inside of her lip as her face heated.

"Angel, you really need to be more careful. I'd hate to have to hurt someone for hurting you."

The heat in her face faded so quickly she had a moment of dizziness and had to grab hold of the door to make sure she didn't go down. Cowboy stepped close and wrapped an arm around her waist.

"Are you okay?"

She blinked a couple times and made sure the world had stopped spinning.

"I'm good. I was just dizzy for a moment. It's passed now."

"You sure you're okay?" A crease formed between his brows.

"It was a passing thing. I'm fine. Are you ready to go?"

"I'm ready when you are, but I want to be sure you're not going to fall off the bike."

Ava shook her head. "I'm fine. It was just a moment. It happens now and then. It's gone now. Do you have someplace in mind for dinner?" She tried to change the subject and get him to move on and forget about that one off-center moment. The last thing she would do was tell him that his instant defense of her was what set it off. No one, except maybe Aaron, had ever defended her so quickly.

Cowboy gave her a look that clearly said she wasn't fooling him, and he wouldn't be letting it go. His arm around her middle loosened slowly, as if making sure she was steady on her feet, then he released her and stepped back to give her a little space.

"I thought we could hit the steak house over on Villard, if steak sounds good to you."

"Steak sounds great. You brought the motorcycle, right?"

"I did. Were you looking forward to riding?"

"I am. I like riding with you."

His face softened and one corner of his mouth curled upward. She wanted to stretch up and kiss those lips, but held back.

"I'm glad to know that. Are you sure you're okay to ride?"

"I'm fine."

His eyes skimmed her from head to toe. "You look all ready, you have your keys?"

"I am and I do, or would you like to come in for a few minutes?" She stepped back to invite him in.

Cowboy shook his head and extended one hand. "No, let's go."

She put her hand in his and stepped out into the hallway, turning to make sure the door was locked, then walked with him down to the parking lot and his motorcycle.

"Need help with the helmet?" Cowboy asked as he handed it to her.

"I think I can get it but if I need help, I'll let you know."

"Okay." He put his on and messed with the bike for a moment.

Ava fumbled with the catch for a moment, until it caught. "I got it!" she didn't bother trying to keep the excitement from her voice.

Cowboy turned back to her with a smile. "Let me check, just to make sure you're safe."

Ava tilted her head back so he could see the clasp. The soft brush of his fingers against her throat sent heat pooling low in her belly. She wasn't sure what he did, but when he spoke again, it came in through the speakers in her helmet.

"You did a great job. It usually takes people longer to get the hang of that." He turned away and threw one leg over the motorcycle. He started and braced it. "Climb on."

He held everything still while Ava carefully put one foot on the peg and swung her leg over the rear of the motorcycle and settled into the seat behind Cowboy, using a hand on his shoulder to stabilize herself. She wrapped her arms around his middle and snuggled close.

"Ready?" He turned his face toward her, though she was sure he couldn't see her with the helmet on.

"Ready."

He walked the motorcycle backwards out of the space, then they zoomed forward as he cranked the accelerator. She found herself grinning as her stomach swooped and flipped then settled as he pulled out onto the street.

When they pulled into the parking lot at the steakhouse a few minutes later, Ava couldn't help but wish the ride had been longer. Cowboy pulled into a space and killed the engine.

"Hungry?" he asked.

"I am." She braced herself on his shoulders and carefully stepped off the motorcycle, then fumbled with the catch on her helmet a moment before finding the release. She lifted the helmet off and handed it to him. "I kind of wish this place was farther from my apartment."

He looked at her a moment, one brow quirked. "Want a longer ride?"

"It would have been nice." She wondered if he might disagree. Was he glad to get her off the back of his motorcycle? She pushed the errant thoughts from her head and focused on him again.

"We can go for a ride after dinner, if you like."

"That would be great."

He put away the helmets in the funny box looking things on either side of the rear wheels, and they went inside.

# 15

A warm feeling of satisfaction settled into Cowboy's chest. He loved that she liked to ride and hoped she would be open to club events. That would let him spend even more time around her. As long as he made sure his brothers knew she was off limits. She was his and there was no way he was sharing.

As they made their way to the table, he glanced over at Ava and wondered if maybe he wasn't getting ahead of himself. He really liked her and wanted to spend a lot more time with her, as long as that was what she wanted too.

He thought he'd told her everything that might change her mind, but after her reaction when he'd picked her up, maybe he'd been wrong. He would need to figure out if there was more she might need to know. Not that he could tell her much about the Kings, and nothing about their business, but he was used to that part.

"What are your plans for this weekend?" he asked once they were seated, and the host had left them.

"I was looking at things to do in the area. You know I haven't been here long. I want to get to know the area. Learn as much as I can about the history and the people here. I think I'm going to hit the museum on Saturday." She paused as the waitress came, brought them water, and took their drink orders. "I wanted to go see the Enchanted Highway, but it seems like a bit of a trip. I'm thinking about waiting until Aaron or Belinda can go with me."

"I've got a ride with the Kings on Saturday, but I'd love to take you down to see the Enchanted Highway on Sunday. We can take the truck or the bike, whichever you're more comfortable with. It will be a pretty long ride."

"I like the idea of taking the motorcycle, but I'm not sure I'm ready to spend all day on it yet. Maybe we should take the truck this time and find a couple of shorter trips so I can work my way up to those longer ones."

"I think I can arrange that." His mind started spinning about what he could do to make a nice trip and cool views into a spectacular trip and a memorable experience for her. "What time would you like to leave?" He didn't know if she planned to attend church anywhere and didn't want to pull her away from something that was likely important to her.

"I'm good with whenever you think is best. I don't know if mornings or afternoon gives better views, but I'm excited either way."

Cowboy tried to remember the way light hit the different sculptures and what might be the best time to see them and how long it would take to get there.

"If you don't have any objections, I'd like to start at about ten."

"Ten is good. What do you want me to bring?"

"You and a jacket in case it gets too windy. I'll take care of everything else." He decided a picnic would be a great plan, and a couple of other stops would make the trip more pleasant.

"I can't wait. What I saw online looks like this will be a great trip."

They turned their attention to the menu, and when the waitress returned with their drinks, ordered.

"Can I ask where you're going Saturday or is that off limits?" she said once the waitress disappeared with their orders.

Cowboy watched her for a moment, trying to decide how much to tell her, and if it would scare her off. After a moment he decided to be as honest as possible. If it scared her off, then he was better off knowing now rather than later.

"Sometimes our events will be secret. Things we can't talk about, other times it won't matter, and we can tell anyone we want. This week is one of the latter. We're taking a ride down to Devil's Tower. You ever seen it?"

"No, what is it?"

"The neck of an ancient volcano, I think. It's pretty cool to see and famous from some old alien abduction movie. I'd love to take you down to see it some time."

"But not Saturday."

"Not Saturday. That's a brothers only ride. Which reminds me. Next weekend is Memorial Day. We're going to have a barbeque. Any way I can convince you to come with me?"

She watched him back for a moment and Cowboy wished he had an idea of what was running through her head.

"Is it an all-weekend thing or just one day?"

"Just one day, I'm sure, but I'm not sure which one. Probably Sunday. Some of our brothers, and some of their families will have to work on Monday, even though that's the holiday."

"I'd like to go, but I need to know which day and what time, so I can rearrange my dinner with Aaron if I need to."

"Do you see him every weekend?"

Ava nodded. "Mostly. This weekend he's out of town. Belinda and I have been doing things during the week instead."

"Sounds like you like your sister-in-law, that's good." He knew a lot of women who hated their brother's spouses and did their best to make things miserable for them. He'd never understood why, only that it happened. He hoped Lisa would like Ava.

"We didn't know each other well for a long time but now that I'm getting to know her, I really like her. She's been welcoming and friendly since I moved to Dickenson. A lot of women would resent a sister, or other family member, suddenly moving to town and needing so much of her husband's attention. Belinda has been great and treats me like her own sister." Ava shook her head as if even she had a hard time believing how much she liked her sister-in-law. Not having any in-laws of his own, at least not yet, Cowboy couldn't relate.

"Anyway," she said with a shake of her head, "I'd love to go with you. Let me know the details and I'll get everything worked out."

"I'll get them no later than Saturday and let you know. Now tell me about your week. What have you been up to?"

They talked until their meals came, then continued to chat through dinner, even sitting a while once they were done. Cowboy liked talking to her. She didn't hesitate to tell him her opinions or even admit that she didn't know anything about whatever subject the conversation had turned to. So many people refused to admit they didn't know what they were talking about that her honesty was refreshing.

By the time he'd paid the tab, and they headed out to the parking lot, Cowboy found himself smiling and wanting more time with her.

"You still want to go for a ride?" he asked as he handed over her helmet.

She held it, watching him for a moment. "If you don't mind, I'd love a bit of a ride."

"What time you want to be home?" He checked his watch.

"I'd like to be home by nine-thirty. That lets me get to bed and get enough sleep for work tomorrow." She slid the helmet onto her head as if she'd done it a hundred times instead of only a few.

That left them with a little over an hour. He could work with that. He put his own helmet on, turned on the radio between his helmet and hers, then got on the bike. After Ava got on behind him, he started the engine and steered them out onto the road. He hadn't had much chance to take her for a ride and while they could ride around town for an hour, he had something else in mind.

# 16

Ava had enjoyed dinner and the conversation they'd had before, during and after. Cowboy was easy to be around, and he didn't condemn her for admitting she didn't know anything about whatever subject had come up. So different from Hank, who'd belittled her if she didn't know something, even if it was some obscure fact she could never have anticipated would come up.

Now, as she sat with her arms around him, Cowboy seemed to be headed out of town. She didn't know where they were headed, and she didn't really care. What mattered to her was that she was here with him, and doing something she was learning to love, something he obviously enjoyed.

She hadn't expected him to pull up onto the interstate, and the speed made her nervous at first, but she soon found herself relaxing against him.

"Where are we going?" she asked after a few minutes.

"It's a surprise. I have something I want to show you. If it were daytime there are other things I'd show you. But it will be dark soon, so that limits things."

She only had more questions, but decided to hold her tongue and see where he was taking her. She'd already admitted she didn't know the area well, so there was no point in trying to figure out what he wanted her to see. Instead, she adjusted her arms around his middle and reveled in the warmth of his back against her front, despite the chill of the wind at this speed.

She'd zoned out and was just enjoying having him close when he steered the motorcycle off the interstate and onto a ramp. Looking around, she noticed lights and buildings that she didn't think she'd ever seen before. He pulled off onto a wide spot in the road near the top of the ramp, killed the engine and took off his helmet. She took that as a sign he was ready to get off. It was a weird place, but she took the hint and carefully stepped off the motorcycle.

She looked around while she waited for him to get off, noticing that she could see lights from miles around.

"I wanted to take you somewhere beautiful, somewhere memorable." Cowboy lifted one shoulder in a half-shrug. "But I didn't want to have to share you with a couple hundred people and it's not the most convenient time of day. This is the tallest place I could drive to in a reasonable amount of time, to show you the lights. It might not seem like there are a lot of people around Dickenson, but when you see it this way, it feels different."

He stepped up behind her and wrapped his arms around her waist. Ava leaned back into his chest, reveling in his warmth and the safe way he made her feel.

"What do you think?"

"It's beautiful." She didn't know what else to say. She'd had no idea how many people were scattered away from the center of town. It made for a stunning light display that nearly took her breath away. She didn't know how long she stood there, taking in the view, but it was long enough, she didn't feel bad turning away from it to spin in Cowboy's arms. She looked up at him for a moment, then spoke.

"Take me home. I've got something I want to show you myself." Hoping he wouldn't misunderstand, she stretched up and kissed him, coaxing his lips open, she tried to pour all she was feeling into that simple, but oh-so-complex touch.

They made it to the door of her apartment. Once inside, Ava turned on him and pushed him back against the door, looking him up and down while giving what she hoped was an almost feral grin.

"Stay," she told him, then stripped out of her jacket and tossed it aside, then turned her attention to him.

She started at his waist, sliding her hands up under the vest he wore, pushing it off his shoulders then tossing it on top of her jacket where it had landed on the seat of a nearby chair, then turning her attention to his shirt.

"Is this what you wanted to show me?"

Ava looked up at Cowboy's face through her lashes, noting that the normally icy green had darkened, she hoped with desire.

"That depends. Do you like it?"

"Do I like a woman who doesn't hesitate to let me know what she wants and doesn't seem to mind taking charge once in a while? Fuck yes. As long as she knows that her being in charge is only in the bedroom, or at least only when it comes to sex."

His gaze raked over her body in a way her body seemed to feel. Her nipples tightened and ached, and heat pooled low in her belly as her core clenched and seemed to throb for a moment in its need to be filled.

"Outside of that, I'm open to discussion, but I won't be led around by the nose, or even by the cock." He met her gaze, as if trying to make sure she understood him.

Words seemed to catch in her throat. She looked down, wondering if she'd gone too far. She'd had one man who had told her what to do and how to do it. She couldn't do that again, she knew.

A finger under her chin brought her gaze back up to meet his. "I don't want to control you. I don't want to stop you from being you. I just want to make sure you're as safe as we can make you. I love watching the way you experience life. The last thing I want to do is break you or your spirit."

Something fluttered in her chest. If she hadn't thought so before, now she knew she was falling in love with him. After her experience with Hank that should terrify her. Oddly though, it was just the opposite. She felt more secure, more anchored.

"In that case, I better make it worth it." Ava tucked her hands under his t-shirt and smoothed them up along his torso to his chest, letting the thin cloth bunch over her hands as she worked her way up his body. "Off," she said when she'd revealed most of his torso.

Without waiting, she bent to flick her tongue back and forth over the tiny button of his nipple.

"Fuck, woman. You're going to drive me out of my mind like that." He tossed the shirt aside. "Angel, let's take this into the bedroom." His hands smoothed up her belly, stirring heat in her core.

Ava let her hands drop to his belt. "I don't care where. I just want you."

"Fuuuck."

There was a thump against the door. Ava jerked her head up. Who was knocking on her door at this hour? Then she realized. It had been Cowboy's head as he let it fall back. She couldn't help the satisfied grin from spreading across her face as she bent to give his other nipple the same attention.

His hands cupped her breasts over her bra, his thumbs flicking across her nipples and drawing a groan from her as she continued to tease him.

Ava couldn't help the small squeak that escaped as he scooped her into his arms.

"Where's the bedroom?" his voice had gone low and rumbly.

Ava pointed to the right doorway, but pressed a kiss against his shoulder as he carried her to the bed.

"There's no way I'm going to take you the first time bent over the back of the sofa, Angel. You're too special for that."

Heat flashed through her. "Bent over the back of the sofa?" The idea had never occurred to her but now that he'd put the idea in her head, she wanted to try it.

"I'm not saying it will never happen, just not for our first time." He set her on the bed and stood.

She watched his gaze skim down her body as he stepped back, then took a seat in the chair in the corner where she liked to sit and read.

"I can't wait to get my hands on you," he said as he bent to unlace his boots. "But I'm going to do this right." He pulled off one boot, then the other dropping them beside the chair before standing again and closing the distance between them. He took Ava's hand and tugged her to her feet before placing a kiss on her lips. Gentle at first then with more feeling and passion.

Ava ran her hands up along his arms then wound them around Cowboy's neck. She tugged him closer and wanted nothing more than to feel his skin against hers.

After a moment she broke the kiss, unwound her arms from around his neck and reached behind her to undo the fastenings at the back of her shirt. She fumbled with the unfamiliar catch and bit back a curse as she couldn't get the thing to release.

"Let me."

Cowboy's patient tone calmed her nerves a little and she turned to let him see the back of her shirt. She picked up her hair off the back of her neck to give him access to the halter as well. No point in only the shirt halfway off.

In seconds, her shirt fell loose. Ava clutched it to her front a moment then shook her head at how stupid she was being.

She'd been trying to take the top off, why was she so desperate to cover herself now?

She turned around and looked up at Cowboy, her face heating.

"You're beautiful." He smoothed the back of one finger down the curve of her cheek. "And if you're not ready, this doesn't have to go any farther."

"No," she reached out and laid one hand on his chest, "don't go. I want this. I'm just, I don't know. It's been a while."

"You're sure?" He watched her with what she felt was concern in his eyes. She fell a little harder in that moment.

"I'm sure." Ava took a deep breath and dropped her top. "Now come here." She grabbed the waistband of his jeans and tugged him closer to her, when he got close enough, she stretched up and kissed him again, eager to let the heady feeling his kisses brought take away her hesitance and embarrassment.

It didn't take long until she forgot her embarrassment and the desire hazing her mind drove her to become more aggressive. She ran her hands up and down his torso, tugging him closer so his chest hair tickled her nipples and only served to make her more eager for him.

Cowboy brought his hands up along her torso, wrapping around her and seeming content to slide along her back. She wanted more.

So much more.

But she didn't know how to ask for it. Hank had never allowed her to be so forward, and had belittled her when she'd tried, telling her it wasn't fitting for a woman of God to be so into sex. Or like it so much.

She pushed thoughts of Hank and what he'd said to her from her mind. He wasn't here, and never would be again. She was moving on and Cowboy seemed to like her just the way she was.

# 17

Something changed. Cowboy noticed the instant her touch became less sure.

"What is it Angel?"

She shook her head. "Nothing that matters."

"If it's messing with your head, it matters. It's okay if you don't want to tell me, though. We'll get there." He smoothed her hair away from her face, and watched her face for signs of whatever was bothering her. He couldn't help but marvel that this woman, who was special in ways he still hadn't explored, wanted him.

She shook her head again. "I'm not going into it, not now. Maybe later, but I have things I want now, and talk isn't one of them." She tugged him close again, and stretched up so her mouth met his.

Cowboy didn't hesitate to kiss her. He loved her taste. The way she seemed to come alive in his arms. She moved against him, her tits rubbing against his chest in a way that made his dick hard.

She seemed to need to take charge here, and he didn't want to take that from her. Instead, he kissed, touched, and encouraged her to take what she wanted.

Slowly, she grew bolder, dipping her fingers below his waistband, then popping the button on his jeans. He covered her hand with his, stopping her progress before she found his hard cock.

"Before things go any farther, I have to ask you something."

"What?" Her voice had grown husky and breathless with desire.

"I hope to God you've got condoms, or I'm going to have to stop right now and go get some. We go much farther, and I won't care. I won't do that to you."

Ava didn't say anything at first, just turned and pulled open the drawer on the table beside the bed, revealing a brand-new value package of condoms.

"I bought them earlier this week when I decided I wanted to see where this was going between us." Ava circled one of her own nipples with the tip of her middle finger.

He watched the pink tip pucker and draw tight, and bit back a groan. He wanted to taste her there so badly, but he was letting her set the pace.

"Good. Now that's out of the way, you can do whatever you want to me. I'm putty in your hands." He released her hand, still on his waistband, and held his hands wide.

"Putty? No, that's soft and squishy and from what I can tell, you're anything but soft and squishy." She unbuttoned his jeans and dipped her fingers beneath the elastic of his boxer briefs. "No, not soft at all." She pushed at his jeans, shoving them off his hips as she leaned close and teased one of his nipples with her tongue a moment before suckling a moment.

Cowboy groaned his head falling back as he fisted his hands and reined in the urge to take over and show her all the things that could bring them both pleasure.

No. There would be plenty of time for that later. Now he was letting her set a pace she was comfortable with. While she hadn't said much, he got the feeling she'd never been allowed to do that before.

He shoved at his jeans until they fell to the floor, then stepped out of them. Ava slid her hands down his sides, skimming over his skivvies, then back up again. She moved around him, her hands on his hips turning her with him, then a firm hand on his chest pushed him backwards until the back of his legs hit the edge of the bed.

"Sit." Ava's tone was firm and commanding.

Cowboy did as she told him, liking the light in her eyes as he followed her commands.

Once he sat on the edge of the bed, she stepped back and slowly unbuttoned her own jeans. He wanted to reach for her, to take over and undress her inch by inch, but held back. Ava shimmied her hips as she pushed the thick cloth down off them. Cowboy's mouth watered. He had to bite back a groan when he noticed she'd caught her panties with her jeans as she'd shed them. For a moment, he wished she'd left them on. He wanted to see her in them, but when she revealed herself to him, a groan escaped anyway. She stood naked in front of him, with a boldness he hadn't expected from her. It made him proud as hell that she felt secure enough to bare herself to him.

Ava stepped out of her jeans and closed the distance between them. With one hand on his chest, she pushed him back until he was lying on the bed, staring up at her and wondering what she would do next.

She gazed at him for a moment, letting her gaze roam down his body and back up again, when it met his, she climbed up onto the bed, one knee on either side of his hips. She hesitated a moment, as if unsure what to do next but her reserve didn't last long. She bent and kissed him again, lightly at first, but it didn't take her long to regain her momentum. Her hands roamed down his body and her knees bent until she all but sat in his lap. While there was no pressure, and only the occasional brush of skin against his underwear, he felt the heat coming from her core where it hovered right above his cock.

Ava broke the kiss and trailed small kisses and gentle love bites down his neck and torso. Cowboy wanted to grab her hips and pull her down against him. To grind that tempting heat against his cock and let her know just what she did to him. No, she would get there eventually. He just had to hold on until then. He ran his hands up her back, then down, let his elbows drop to the bed as his finger skimmed around to her belly, then slowly moved up. She'd long since taken off her shirt and given what they were in the middle of, he hoped she wouldn't be offended as he moved his hands up to cup her breasts.

The soft mounds filled his hands, he wanted to lean up and take the tips into his mouth but couldn't with her swirling her tongue down his abdomen. Instead, he let his head fall back against the bedspread and teased her nipples with his thumbs while he gently kneaded her tits.

Ava set her teeth into the skin at his hip and bit down. He hoped that meant she liked what he was doing, that it was doing things for her. The way she worked her way down his body was doing things for him. His dick throbbed as he thought about where she was headed and the idea of her mouth on his cock nearly had him coming then and there. His mind flashed back to when he'd been in the shower, imagining her on her knees, his cock in her mouth.

Holy shit, he needed to think about something else.

# 18

Ava hoped she was doing this right. She loved the way Cowboy's hands felt on her body, but other than a few groans, she hadn't gotten any reaction from him as she'd used her mouth to work her way down his body.

When she reached the waistband of his underwear she hesitated. Hank had never let her do this to him. She knew most men seemed to like it, some begged for it, and she'd always wondered what it was like, but where did she go from here?

She ran her hand over his underwear, along the length of his erection, marveling for a moment how something could change so much.

"Um, Angel?" Cowboys voice had gone rough and breathy.

"Yeah?" She stayed bent low over his groin and looked up at him through her lashes.

"As much as I'm enjoying what you're doing, we need to pull out one of those condoms, and I'd prefer not to come in your mouth the first time, which I will if you go much farther where you're headed."

She didn't say anything, just continued to watch him.

"What I'd really love is if you'd let me wrap it up, then you would come up here and ride me."

Heat washed through her body at his words. The image of her kneeling astride him, her back arched and her own hands toying with her breasts flashed through her mind.

"Ride you? You'd let me do that?"

"I'd let you do nearly anything you want. I'd love to see you ride me." His green eyes had darkened to a deep emerald and his thumbs flicked across her nipples sending a frisson of pleasure through her.

She sat up, then leaned toward the still open table drawer to pull out the box of condoms. She wanted to whimper as her movements pulled her breasts out of his reach.

Box in hand she fumbled with it, trying to open the plastic seal wrapped around the box. After a moment she growled, bit the plastic, and ripped it off. She didn't bother trying to open the box neatly, instead ripped the top off and pulled out a string of foil-wrapped sheaths. She dropped the string on the bed beside Cowboy and shoved the box onto the table.

By the time she'd turned back to Cowboy, he'd picked up the string, ripped one off and torn it open. He lifted his hips, shoved his boxer briefs down to where her legs rested on either side of his, and was unrolling the condom down his length.

As she watched him, trepidation filled her anew. She'd only ever been with Hank, who had sworn his manhood was large, but Cowboy's was bigger. She had no doubt it would fit, but she wondered if it might hurt as she stretched to fit him.

He finished with the condom then lay back and curled his fingers at her in a come-hither motion. Ava couldn't help the smile that curved her lips as she put her hands on his stomach and let them slide up his body as she leaned forward. She teased his nipples a moment, laving first one then the other with her tongue, before she crawled up his body, noticing how his erection slide along her skin as she moved, until they were face to face and his dick was lined up with her opening.

She kissed him again, letting the heat that always built between them wash away her inhibitions. Then she rocked back until he was pressed against her core and sat upright, letting her weight push her down over him. As she moved, she let her hands slide down his torso, then pulled them up her thighs and continued up her own torso. She cupped her own breasts for a moment before lightly pinching her nipples. A whimper escaped her throat as her hips met his. She was a little surprised there was no pain, but also filled with elation.

"God you're beautiful." Cowboy's hands came to rest on her thighs as she lifted herself up a couple inches, then sank back down over him once more. It took her a moment to find a rhythm, and only a couple moments longer to realize it wasn't her hands she wanted on her breasts, but his. She picked up his hands from where they rested on her thighs and brough them to her breasts.

When he covered them, squeezing then tweaking her nipples as if he knew exactly what she needed. Sensation overwhelmed her. Her body seemed to clench and a feeling she didn't recall having ever felt before washed through her. She bit her bottom lip to keep from begging for more as her toes curled. Ava let her head fall back but kept moving. Whatever that feeling filling her body was, she needed more.

Cowboy's thumb on her chin made her straighten and look at him, her hips still rocking against his.

"Don't hold it in, Angel. I want to hear every gasp and moan."

"I don't know if I can do that," she said, barely able to get the words out between breaths.

His hands went to her hips, guiding her to move just a little faster.

"You can do it. Just don't think about it."

She met his pace. He moved his hands from her hips back to her breasts and flicked and pinched her nipples. Heat raced through her. She couldn't stop the cries of pleasure that escaped from her lips.

"More. Please, more."

He rolled her nipples between her fingers sending bolts of heat to pool low in her belly.

Ava didn't know what was happening to her, only that she didn't want it to stop. The heat in her belly intensified, seeming to boil over, then exploded through her body. Her toes curled, she gripped Cowboy's arms where he still cupped and played with her breasts, afraid she would fly away. A cry escaped her lips as her whole body seemed to clench and seize.

She didn't know how long it lasted, only that when her body relaxed and she once more became aware of her surroundings, Cowboy still held her, still teased her nipples.

"I like hearing that, Angel. It tells me you're getting what you need."

"What was that?" Her voice shook.

Cowboy froze. His fingers stopped playing back and forth over her breasts and his hips stilled beneath her.

"Angel," his voice had changed but she didn't have the presence of mind to figure out how or what that meant right now, "please tell me you didn't just say what I think you said?"

Ava blinked; her mind still sluggish. It took a moment for his words to process.

"What do you think I said?" She frowned down at where his gaze seemed to be locked on her face.

He closed his eyes and took several deep breaths. She didn't know if he was looking for patience or trying to regain his composure and control.

"While those weren't your words, I think you just told me that after I don't know how many years of marriage, that was your first orgasm."

"Orgasm? No. I'm sure I've had those before."

"But you didn't know what that was."

"Is that what that was?" Ava frowned, confused. She'd always enjoyed sex with her ex, enough that he'd told her frequently that it was inappropriate for his wife to like it. She was supposed to see it as a duty to him. "Obviously, I was wrong. I've never experienced anything like that before." She felt her lips curve into a smile as she leaned down over him, shivering briefly at the way he felt still buried deep inside her. "I'm glad you were the one to show me how amazing it feels though." She kissed the tip of his nose then rocked her hips against his.

He groaned and his hands, which hadn't left her breasts as she'd moved, began to knead the sensitive mounds again. "I think I may have created a monster."

"Not possible. I can't be both an angel and a monster."

"Sure you can. You may be the sexiest fallen angel I've ever seen."

Ava's breath caught in her throat as his arms moved around her and he rolled them both until she lay on her back, staring up at him.

"I can't wait to complete your corruption." He moved inside her, stopping any protest she might have had, then making her forget it, if there had been one.

# 19

Cowboy woke curled on one side, one arm folded and tucked under his head, the other wrapped snuggly around Ava.

Damn it felt good to wake up with her in his arms. He would love to find a way for this to happen more often. He knew he needed to get moving, he had things he needed to get done today. But he hadn't planned to start the day here or like this. Not that he was complaining. far from it.

No. Waking this way made him want to repeat it — every day if he could. That was unlikely, at least at this stage, but it was a nice thought. A glance at the clock on the table beside the bed told him it was earlier than he'd thought. He had more time to enjoy the moment with Ava than he'd initially thought. He looked back down at where she lay curled in his arms and found her awake, her eyes on him.

"How long have you been watching me?" he asked.

"Not long. How long have you been awake?"

"Not long." He resisted the urge to grin as he turned her words back on her.

She blinked, as if not sure how to take him or how to respond.

"I was thinking I need to take a shower before I get ready for work and that maybe you'd like to join me."

She lowered her eyes in what from anyone else he would take as being coy or flirting, but he'd learned that from Ava it was another gesture of her uncertainty.

He'd like to get five minutes alone with her ex. Five minutes was all it would take to readjust his views on how to treat a woman. especially one as precious as Ava.

"Are you sure you're not sore, you said it had been a while. I don't want to hurt you."

"I'm fine." She blushed and Cowboy wasn't sure if it was from embarrassment or desire, but he wasn't going to push the issue. If she said she was fine, he would take her word for it.

"I can think of lots of ways to make a shower fun." He loosened his hold on her as she stretched then rolled for the edge of the bed to get up. Without her there to lure him into staying, he threw back the covers and stood. "What time do you need to leave so you're not late?"

She gave him a time, then went into the attached bathroom, not seeming to notice she had not a stitch on. He looked around for his clothes, went to the front room for his t-shirt, then left them all draped over the chair next to his boots before joining her in the shower.

***

Cowboy found his mind drifting more and more. Thinking both about the night before with Ava and looking forward to seeing her again tonight.

Before he'd left her this morning, they'd made plans for dinner then back to her place tonight. He could only imagine what she had in mind. Those imaginings were not good for his concentration. The upside was that the assembly he was working on didn't take a lot of detailed focus, and his musings didn't hinder getting things done.

"Cowboy!" Deke's voice pulled him from his thoughts. His best friend's tone hinted that this might not be the first time he'd called his name.

"You need something?" He turned and glared at his VP. The last thing he wanted right now was the other man to realize his mind had been on Ava again. He didn't want to hear the teasing that would be sure to follow.

"Miles has been trying to reach you all morning. He needs some decisions about tomorrow. Says you're not responding to texts."

Cowboy hadn't even noticed his phone buzzing. He'd been so lost in what he'd been doing and his thoughts. He pulled out his phone and found several texts from Miles, and one from Ava. Ignoring that Deke was watching him, he went to Ava's message first.

**Ava:** *Have a good day. I'll be thinking about you. Until tonight.*

He typed out a quick reply and hit send, then navigated to Miles messages. Sure enough, there were several questions that Cowboy typed out answers to and sent back to him. When he was done with all the texting, he looked up to find Deke still watching him, his head tilted to one side and one brow lifted.

"What?" Cowboy demanded. Something smart mouthed or snarky was going to come out of Deke's mouth, he had no doubt.

"I didn't know questions about a run would put that stupid grin on your face."

"It wasn't just questions from Miles waiting for me. I had other messages too."

"From that hot little number from the bar last week? You've seen her a couple times since then, haven't you?"

"I have." At least his brother wasn't calling her a piece of ass this time. He could handle hot little number. It wasn't so demeaning. But if Deke got too flippant, Cowboy might have to teach him some manners. "And I'm seeing her again tonight. I may even end up bringing her next weekend." Cowboy watched his friend, wanting to see how he would react.

Deke's brows shot up, then he gave Cowboy a long blink before speaking, "You're going to bring this chick to the club BBQ? She looked a little wild, but I didn't take her for a groupie."

Cowboy pinned him with a venomous look. "Ava is no groupie. She'd never been on a bike until this week." He'd stepped in it now. Jumping to her defense like that would clue Deke in that there was something special about Ava. The surprised look on his brother's face made that more than clear. Now the ribbing would start.

"You're going to bring a woman who's new to the world to the BBQ?"

"Maybe. She said she was interested, but I need to get some details from Miles so she can work out the scheduling." That reminded him and he pulled out his phone and texted Miles again, asking what day the BBQ would be on the next weekend. He'd told Ava he'd find out Saturday, but if he could find out today, that would give her an extra day.

"You almost done with this rig?" Deke jerked his chin toward the bike Cowboy had been working on.

"Getting close. And it's a good thing. The buyer will be here tomorrow, and I'd like to take it out for a test drive this afternoon to make sure there are no issues."

"Good plan. Want a partner?"

"For the test drive? I'd appreciate it. It's been a while since one broke down on the ride, but it's always a pain in the ass when you have to wait for rescue. At least with you along I'll have someone to wait with."

Deke shook his head. "What time you want to leave?"

"About two. I want to make it a decent ride, give this thing time to even out and break in a little. That good for you?" He looked up from where he was connecting wires to watch his VP's reaction.

"Two is good. Make sure you answer your messages from Miles. He gets a little pissy when you don't."

Cowboy nodded, his attention back to the work he was doing on the bike. He needed to stay busy on it if he was going to be done in time to take it out with Deke.

Deke hung around for a few more minutes, then left, headed back over to the clubhouse, Cowboy assumed, but he hadn't asked. His mind had already skipped past the test drive and was on Ava and his plans for tonight.

# 20

Ava's day seemed to crawl by. Not because she wasn't busy, she was. But it wasn't what she wanted to be doing. She'd hated watching Cowboy leave that morning, even knowing she'd see him again in a few hours.

Nor could she not keep him off her mind, but every time she moved, her body reminded her of all the delicious ways he'd shown her to find pleasure. She had several aches and possibly a couple of bruises, not that she regretted a single second of it. Every twinge and throb were a reminder and she wanted to close her eyes and relive every moment, not that she had time to indulge.

Finally, at the end of the day, she clocked out and headed out to the car, digging in her purse for her keys and phone as she walked. When she reached the car, she started it and sat inside with the door open, scanning her messages while she waited for the AC to cool down.

She frowned at the screen when she saw a message from Aaron. He didn't text her often. She wondered what he wanted. When she opened the message, she stared at the screen for several seconds.

**Aaron:** *WHY AM I JUST FINDING OUT NOW THAT YOU'RE DATING A BIKER. HOW COULD YOU BE SO IRRISPONSIBLE. WE WILL BE TALKING ABOUT THIS. CALL ME.*

He didn't text her often enough to know if this was just how he used his phone. She didn't think so but would hate to jump to the wrong conclusion.

Ava closed the door, dialed Belinda, and put the car in gear, knowing the call would go over the speakers in the car.

"Hey, you must have just gotten out of work. What's up?"

"Is Aaron still out of town?"

"Yeah, he won't be home until the middle of next week, why?"

"I got a text from him while I was at work. He doesn't text me often. Does he often leave it on caps when he texts?"

Belinda was quite a moment. "Um. No. He is usually really careful not to do that. What did he send you?"

"He found out about Cowboy and is apparently not happy I'm dating a biker."

"I'm so sorry. I didn't know it was a secret. It came up when I talked to him this morning, and I told him what you'd told me."

"No worries. It isn't a secret. I'd just not told him until I decided I was going to keep seeing Cowboy, and the subject hadn't come up since then."

"I'm sorry he shouted at you over text. I'm even more sorry it's my fault." Belinda's voice was sincere.

Ava didn't blame her but now that she knew she hadn't taken her brother's text wrong, she needed to figure out how she was going to respond to him.

She chatted with Belinda for a few more minutes, then rang off just before she got home. She had a few things she wanted to get done before Cowboy arrived. One of them was contacting Aaron.

Inside, she put away her bag and headed into the bedroom to change clothes. On the way, she typed up her text to her brother.

**Ava:** *Yes, I'm dating a biker. We can discuss it after you get home, and only if you're going to be an adult. I will not listen to you yell at me over my choices.*

She stared at the screen a moment after she hit send, wondering if she'd done the right thing. Then she added another message and hit send.

**Ava:** *and no, I'm not going to stop seeing him just because you don't like the idea. It would have to be some damning evidence about him specifically. Or you can meet him and maybe get to know him. Like an adult.*

With that chore done, she tossed her phone on the bed and peeled out of her work clothes. She stood in front of her closet for a couple of minutes, trying to decide what to wear. She wanted to be comfortable, but she also wanted to look nice for Cowboy.

After a bit she settled on a pair of shorts and a tank top, opting to go barefoot because her feet ached. She'd just finished dressing when someone knocked on her door. A glance at the bedside clock told her it was a quarter to six. A little early for Cowboy, but not out of the question.

At the door, she assumed it was Cowboy and opened it without checking to see who it was. It wasn't until she stepped back to let him in that she realized the man on the other side of the door wasn't Cowboy.

The man standing there was someone she didn't recognize and didn't think she'd ever seen before. She stepped forward, pulling the door from all the way open, hoping to keep him from stepping inside.

"Can I help you?" She did her best to keep her tone polite, but something about him set off alarm bells in her mind.

"You sure can, sweetheart. You can come with me."

Before Ava had a chance to tell him no or close the door, he pushed his way inside. He grabbed one arm and twisted it behind her so that ever time she moved or tried to fight, a shooting pain shot through her shoulder.

"What's going on? Why are you doing this?"

"They messed with the wrong man. I'm going to teach them a lesson." The stranger kept his hold on her arm as he steered her down the hall and into the elevator. Then out of the building and into the parking lot. She didn't see anyone around.

Why was there no one around when she needed them? What would Cowboy think when he found her apartment door standing open and her nowhere to be found?

These thoughts and a million more raced through her head as he forced her into the back seat of a car that had been idling in a parking space, then followed her into the seat. There was another man in the driver's seat and as soon as the door closed, the car backed out of the space and left.

Why hadn't she listened to Cowboy and checked who was at the door before opening it?

# 21

Cowboy had just pulled into the parking lot and was in the middle of pulling the food he'd picked up on the way over from the saddle bags on his bike when a noise caught his attention. He looked up to see Ava stepping out the front door. Her posture and the expression on her face told him something was wrong. He stepped behind the cab of a pickup parked next to him just in time to see Rooster step out behind her, one arm bent up behind her back.

Rage washed through Cowboy. He nearly stepped out to confront the man he used to call brother, but reason intervened. Rooster wouldn't do this on his own. He wasn't smart enough to plan this on his own. If Rooster was involved, Jonesy would be nearby and, in all likelihood, Tank was pulling their strings. He needed to keep his cool and follow them.

The last thing he wanted was to pull Ava out of this but leave an element of the group free to target her again. He watched as Rooster pushed her into the back seat of an older model sedan he didn't know if he'd ever seen before. He followed her into the rear seat then the car backed out.

Cowboy didn't wait for them to leave before stepping out from behind the truck. He went to his bike, closed the saddlebags from where he'd left them open, and stepped astride the bike. As the car came toward him, he realized Jonesy was behind the wheel. It only took him a moment to start the bike then he waited for them to pull out of the complex parking lot before pulling out and following them. He needed to know where they were going, but he didn't want to be too close. He didn't want them to know he was on their tail.

At the first stoplight that turned red, Cowboy activated the Bluetooth in his helmet and told his phone to dial Deke.

"I thought you were spending the evening with your girl?" Deke said as he answered his phone. "What are you doing calling me?"

"We've got a problem."

"Talk."

"I arrived at Ava's in time to see Rooster walk her out and force her into a car." The light turned green, Cowboy continued through traffic, keeping several cars between him and the sedan, but not letting the sedan, and Ava, out of his sight. "It looked like he had her in a hammer lock. As soon as they were both in the car, the car left. I'm tailing it now. Jonesy is driving and Rooster is in the back seat with her. We're headed west on 9th Street between 4th Ave and Sims. I don't know where they're headed, but it wouldn't be a bad idea to have some back up."

"I'm on it. I've texted Miles and Caden. They're the only two I trust a hundred percent not to have some allegiance to these two or Tank. What are they driving? If I can get one or both of them out to you, they can take your place and let you fall back so they don't spot you."

He gave the description of the vehicle, even down to the license plate when he got close enough to read it before falling back again. As much as Cowboy hated to admit it, even to himself, someone to help tail them would be helpful. He didn't want to let the car, and Ava out of his sight, but who knew what Rooster and Jonesy would do to her if they spotted him. Who knew what they had planned? He hoped it was some kind of ransom plan, but after what they'd pulled with that other club a few months ago, he couldn't count on it. He wasn't willing to risk Ava's safety on it.

Deke kept talking to him over the headset in his helmet as Cowboy followed them. A few minutes later his VP let him know that Caden was right behind him in a pickup, he could peel off the pursuit and they wouldn't lose them.

It went against every instinct, but he took the next right, turning off the trail and looping back around. He pulled back onto 9$^{th}$ Street about a half mile behind where he'd turned off, waiting for news that it was his turn to tail them or that they'd stopped somewhere. Deke was still on the phone, keeping him on top of what was going on, giving him directions as they turned from one street to another.

After about a mile, Miles took Caden's place following the car. It was Miles that saw it turn into a warehouse lot, then disappear through one of the overhead doors.

"Fuck," Cowboy said as he cranked the accelerator. He needed to be there now. Who knew what these twatwaffles had planned for her. It could be something as simple as ransoming her back to him, or so much worse. Especially if, as he suspected, Tank was calling the shots.

The bike shot forward as rage once again filled him. He had to get there and save her. He could only hope this wouldn't scare her off because damned if he hadn't gone and fallen in love with her, despite knowing better.

# 22

Ava could barely think. Terror filled her mind. Who were these men and what did they want with her? Once she was in the car and the car moving, they didn't seem to worry much about her. They talked between them.

It took her a few minutes for the panic and terror that had kept her from noticing much to fade.

Slowly, she became aware of what was being said around her.

"How did an asshole like him get a girl that pretty?" the driver asked, leering at her in the rear-view mirror.

"Don't know and don't care. I just care that he gives us what we deserve," the one who'd pulled her from her apartment said.

She thought of him as Jerkface. The driver could be Butthead.

It took a moment to realize they were talking about Cowboy. What did he have to do with these two? And why did they want her? Had he done something to anger them? Or was it something else?

She hadn't seen him as they had come out of the apartment building and she didn't have her phone, as she'd left it in the kitchen. There was no way for him to find her.

The car made several turns and she soon lost track of where they were. She still had no clue where they'd taken her when they pulled the car into a building. The interior was dark until the driver, the man she thought of as Butthead, opened his car door. Not that the interior light of the car illuminated much. She thought about pushing open the door and making a run for it, but between being in a dark building and having no idea where the doors were and not knowing where in town she was, she decided it would be better to wait.

"Don't even think about running," Jerkface said, as if reading her mind. "We're being nice to you so far. Make things too hard on us and we can get ugly."

Ava didn't know what to say to that, she wasn't going to deny she'd been thinking about running. If she had a choice she wasn't going to say anything. Why let them know how terrified she was? She wasn't going to think about what he meant by 'ugly' either.

The last thing she wanted to do was to give them more power or leverage over her. Well, other than their having kidnapped her. She still didn't know why they'd taken her. Surely there was a better target when it came to getting Cowboy's attention. Why would you take a girl he'd been seeing only a week?

She wondered again why she was here.

A bright overhead light came on, making her wince as it stung her eyes.

"Get a move on," Jerkface said from beside her.

She'd been hiding her eyes and hadn't noticed Butthead opening the door beside her. Jerkface shoved at her until she slid out of the vehicle, then followed, so she had one man in front of her and another behind. There was only one direction she could go so she took a step toward the back of the car, trying to get enough space so neither stood in her personal space.

"Oh no you don't." Jerkface grabbed her arm and twisted it behind her again.

Ava clenched her teeth to keep from crying out, but didn't say anything. He steered her to an office chair that had seen better days against one wall, then shoved her as they approached. The seat was torn and there was at least one missing wheel.

"Sit. If you're good, I'll leave you loose. If you move, we'll tie you to it."

She sat and was thankful she wasn't on the floor or some filthy mattress as she watched the two of them move to the far side of what looked like a warehouse. There were a few crates stacked against one wall, the car they'd come in, and a lot of dust.

The two men talked, but they were far enough away she could only pick up a word here and there. She caught call, ransom, pay. She thought they were talking about Cowboy, or maybe Aaron? Had her brother pissed someone off by selling them a bad car? But why take her like this? There had to be legal protections in place for something like that. She didn't think it was Aaron they were talking about and the only person she could think of it might be, was Cowboy. Or maybe they had the wrong person. What would happen to her if she wasn't the person they'd meant to take?

Ava hoped someone would figure out where she was and do something to get her free. She eyed the men still across the huge room, then looked toward the door they'd driven in through. It was closed now and there was no way for her to get it open. Beside it was a regular-sized door. But what if it was locked? With the way were taking turns keeping an eye on her, there was no way she'd make it out. There was another regular sized door on the far side of the building from where they'd come in, but where did it go?

She could try for either one, but now she was loose and at least mostly comfortable. She didn't want to get tied to the chair, just in case something happened to distract them, and she got the chance to make a run for it.

# 23

Cowboy was ready to hit the rolling door at full speed, burst through it and take Ava back. It took both Miles and Caden blocking him and his bike from getting to the warehouse to get him to stop. Then all three, including Deke, who had arrived moments after he had, to talk some sense into him.

He didn't care if it was the smart move. He wanted her back. Now.

He wanted to be sure they hadn't hurt her.

Once they'd convinced him to stop and think things through, he parked his bike and stood in a pool of shadows beside Miles' pickup about a quarter mile down the street from the warehouse where they'd taken Ava.

They exchanged ideas, Cowboy never taking his eyes off the door where they'd taken her.

"They're not dumb enough to hurt her," Deke said. "Not without making their demands first. They'll give you a chance to give them what they want before they get too rough."

"It's the difference between their definition of too rough and mine that I'm worried about. Ava is sweet. She's innocent. She's not the kind of girl they spend time with." He shook his head and glared at the warehouse, vowing they would pay for every mark they left on her.

They were still discussing the options when his phone rang. He wanted to pick it up and demand they give Ava back now, but that wouldn't do any good.

Cowboy clenched his teeth and took a deep breath before picking up the call, putting it on speaker so the other men could hear what was being said.

"This is Cowboy," It took everything in him to keep his voice calm and tone even.

"Are you missing something?" Rooster's voice came across the line.

"Yes, and she better be unharmed when you give her back. What do you want?"

"Drop the charges against Tank. Give him, and us, back our positions."

Deke rolled his eyes. Miles scowled and Caden just looked confused.

Cowboy fought not to laugh. His demands were never going to happen. The charges against Tank were county charges, there was nothing Cowboy or any of the Kings could do about them. The police had found enough evidence in Tank's house to put him away for years. It was likely that Rooster and Jonesy would do some time too. His mind flashed on the face of the biker they'd captured and beaten which had ended in these charges and his stomach flipped. Would they try to do the same to Ava?

If they did, he would have a lot more to do with charges than he did now. And maybe a little personal revenge too.

"That's going to take some time. I have to reach out to a lot of people and get some gears moving. All the offices are closed for the weekend."

"You have twenty-four hours."

"How do I know you haven't already killed her and are just stringing me along?" Cowboy clenched his teeth again at the idea.

"Come on, sweetheart, talk to your boyfriend. Tell him you're okay," Rooster's voice was replaced by another.

"Cowboy?" Ava's voice shook, but it was strong, not like she was hurt.

"Yeah, Angel, it's me. Are you hurt?"

"I'm not hurt. What's going on?"

"Nothing that you've done and I'm going to—" Before he had a chance to continue, Rooster came back on the line.

"You know she's good, now get Tank free, and our positions back, or your girlfriend isn't going to be so pretty." The call disconnected.

Cowboy's gaze flicked from man to man before going back to the warehouse.

"They've lost their minds," Miles said after a moment.

"We can't get the charges dropped," Deke said. "And they were voted out of the club. This won't get them back in."

"I know." Cowboy took a deep breath. "We have to figure out how to get in there and get her out. Sooner rather than later. They're expecting things to take time, they're not expecting us to go in and get her back. The longer things take, the more risks they'll take, and the more likely they are to get bored and hurt Ava. I'm not willing to risk that."

They stood, the other men watching him for several moments before anyone spoke.

"We need something to draw them out," Miles was the first one to speak. "Something to make them leave her alone in there. Then one of us could slip in and grab her."

"I have to be the one to go in," Cowboy said. "She doesn't know any of you. It would be just like these cocksuckers taking her." He took a deep breath and forced himself to let it out slowly, hoping it would help his brain function in something less than panic mode.

He was better under pressure than this. He hadn't even panicked like this when Tank had been arrested and he had to hold the Kings together. He was better than this. He just had to pull himself together and get past the fact that it was Ava they had.

"All right. Give me some thoughts on ways to get them out of the building?" He looked from face to face of the men surrounding him.

They threw out several ideas, but nothing Cowboy thought would work.

"We could get the police involved," Caden said. "We have an eyewitness that they took her against her will and that they are in that building with her. It might be enough to get them to go in. Once they're in they'll ask her if she's there willingly. Would she say yes?"

"I can't imagine that she would, but who knows what they've told her. What if they tell her if she says no, they'll kill her?" Cowboy shook his head. "I can't risk it."

"What do we know about that building?" Deke spoke up.

"Not a lot. I've never been here before," Caden said.

"I have, but I'm not sure I can tell you much more. It's a warehouse. Last time I was here there were a few crates inside. I never had a chance to see what was in them. Tank and Rooster kept some things inside. A fishing boat, a couple cars. I imagine most of that has been sold off to pay legal expenses, but who knows," Miles said.

"What else can you tell us?" Deke turned to Miles. "Doors, weapons, anything?"

"I never saw any weapons inside, but who knows what's in those crates? But they could have brought weapons in with them. As for doors. There's a standard door next to the overhead and another standard on the opposite wall. Both lead outside."

"When were you here?" Cowboy asked with a frown, trying to remember why they might have brought him out here.

"Last year, just after I came back. I didn't know Tank or the others well, they seemed to be testing me. I'm not sure if they didn't like what they found or they did. Either way, I'm glad they didn't pull me into their stupid stunt with that other club."

"Have you seen the other side of the building?" Deke asked. "Anything blocking that door? How sure are you it leads outside."

"The door was open last time I was here, all of them were. I can't say there's nothing blocking it now, as it's been so long, but there wasn't then."

"Good to know," Cowboy said looking around the small group of men. "I can go in that door if we can find a way to get them outside or at least to the other end of the warehouse. I wish we knew where in the building they were keeping Ava."

"I think you're the best way to get them out of there. Is there anything one of us could take in to let her know she's safe with us, that you sent us?" Deke watched him. "They won't think you're up to something if you show up demanding to see them. And it's soon enough they may not think you've called in back up already. Besides, I'm better with lockpicks than you are."

Cowboy shot his best friend a look and slowly nodded once. He never would have admitted Deke was better than him, except this was Ava's safety, and possibly her life. He hated to admit it, but he had no idea how far these two fuckers would go to get what they wanted.

They spent another twenty minutes putting together a plan, then Cowboy, Deke and the others got into place. Deke at the back of the warehouse with his lockpicks, Miles and Caden on either side of the front door, and Cowboy ready to pull his bike up out front and confront Rooster and Jonesy.

He could only hope things went as planned.

# 24

Ava didn't know how long she'd been sitting in the decrepit office chair. Jerkface and Butthead had spent most of the time since they'd put her in this chair huddled on the far end of the building. She would have thought they were ignoring her, but every time she shifted in the chair or even twisted it a little bit, a head shot up and Jerkface gave her a warning look. Butthead looked at her differently. His looks sent a shiver of fear down her spine.

She did not want to be left alone with him. He gave her the creeps and she could tell he had something planned that she would not enjoy. Not that she was enjoying sitting here but at least she wasn't being hurt. She wasn't sure that would remain true if she was alone with Butthead.

A loud rumble came from the front of the warehouse, or at least what she thought was the front. The same side they'd come in from. It seemed to vibrate the whole building, making her pull her hands up to cover her ears. There was shouting from outside that she couldn't make out.

Butthead went to the normal door beside the one they'd driven in through and stepped outside. There was more shouting, this time she could tell it was Butthead, though his words didn't carry.

Jerkface glared at her. He pointed as if telling her to stay put, then followed Butthead to the door and out.

Was now her chance to run? She could go to the door at the far end of the warehouse, but what if it just led into another room? She'd be trapped, they would find her, drag her back to the chair and tie her down. Maybe something worse.

She didn't want to think about the something worse.

The vibrations stopped. She hazarded removing her hands from her ears. There was shouting going on outside, but she couldn't make out what was being said.

Ava had to bite back a scream, though she nearly jumped through the roof when someone appeared beside her. He had tattoos on both arms and rings on nearly every finger. His hair and beard were well trimmed and neat, though they'd gone to salt and pepper that didn't match his skin. She leaned away from him, not sure what was going on.

"My name is Deacon. Cowboy sent me to get you out of here."

"Why didn't he come himself?" She kept her voice soft, following the stranger's example. How was she to know this guy wasn't in league with Butthead and or Jerkface and trying to trick her?

"Several reasons, number one being it was a better use of resources to put him out front to distract your kidnappers. He also said to tell you that he calls you Angel and that he's planning to take you to see the Enchanted Highway on Sunday, to prove to you I'm who I say."

Ava sent the main door, where her captors had disappeared a glance then pushed out of the chair.

"Let's go." She followed the stranger out the door she'd seen earlier and didn't know where it led. It stood open now, showing it led outside. How had she not noticed him opening it?

Because her attention had been on what was going on outside, that's why. She headed for the door, and he fell in behind her. As soon as they were outside, he closed the door and pulled out his phone. She let him take the lead, showing her where to go, while his fingers flew over the screen on his phone.

"This way." Deacon kept his voice low while he led her around one side of the warehouse. She didn't see anyone, but followed without a word. He was her best chance to get out of there, and she didn't want to screw things up.

# 25

It went against everything in him to stand there arguing with these fuckheads when all he wanted to do was knock their heads together and race past them to get to Ava. But Cowboy forced himself to follow the plan.

Deke would get her out of there if he had to throw her over his shoulder and haul her out. Cowboy hoped he didn't have to do that. Mostly because of how badly it might scare her.

He was still arguing with Rooster when Miles signaled to him from the corner of the building that Ava was safe. That was the end of Cowboy's patience. He closed the distance between himself and Rooster and with a single punch to the face, knocked the other man to the ground.

Miles and Caden closed in on Jonesy from behind, taking him down and pinning him to the ground.

"Call the police. Now that Ava's safe, we do this right. I'll testify even if she won't." He turned to go get Ava from where they'd agreed Deke would take her once he got her out, but found her on her way to him. He wasn't sure when, but she'd come around the corner and was now running for him.

She ran into him and threw her arms around his neck. He held her close, letting her catch her breath. When she lifted her head from where she'd buried it against his chest, he searched her face for any sign they'd been rougher on her than they'd had to be.

"Are you okay? Did they hurt you?"

She shook her head. "I'm fine. I wasn't even tied to the chair." She inhaled a shaky breath. "If I'd have been braver, I would have tried to walk out sooner. But they threatened to tie me down or let things get 'ugly'." She dropped her face to his chest again, seeming to take a deep breath as she hugged him closer. "I'm so glad to see you. Do you know them?" She pulled away to look down at the men who were still on the ground, Miles and Caden each having pinned one down while he'd been distracted by Ava.

"I do. I'm sorry you got mixed up in this. If I'd known they would do something so stupid I would have warned you. We've already called the police, but I saw them take you and there was no way I was going to wait to make sure they weren't hurting you." He wrapped an arm around her waist and pulled her close.

"You saw them take me? How? I looked for you and didn't see you."

"I saw you come out of the building, and I could tell there was something wrong by the way you walked. I didn't know who it was or that it was about me until they passed me pulling out of the parking lot. I followed. There was no way I was going to sit there waiting for the police while they took you God knows where."

"I'm glad you didn't." She hugged him.

A police car pulled in, followed by a second. They spent the next hour answering questions and repeating what had happened.

# 26

By the time Ava made it home she was shaking with exhaustion and stress. She was ready to collapse and sleep for a week. She knew that wouldn't happen, but at least tomorrow was Saturday and she had no plans.

"Come sit down for a few minutes. I'll heat this stuff up and at least we can eat."

Cowboy guided her to the sofa where she sat while he carried the food he'd pulled from the things on his motorcycle into the kitchen. She didn't know if she would be able to eat but she would try.

While he was gone, she stared at the wall, trying to process what had happened. She'd been terrified, but they hadn't hurt her. But there was nothing saying she wouldn't be hurt next time. Could she handle a next time?

Her mind went blank. She didn't want to think about something like this happening again.

"Here's your plate." Cowboy came into the room carrying a pair of plates. "You want to eat in here or in the kitchen?"

"In the kitchen." She pushed herself to her feet and followed him to the other room.

They sat at the kitchen table, Ava ate mechanically, barely registering what they were eating. Something was off, but she couldn't say exactly what.

When they were done, Cowboy cleaned up, putting their dishes in the dishwasher, and wiping down the counters before he went to the table where Ava still sat.

"Come on, Angel. Let's go lay down."

"I don't know. I'm not sure I'm in the mood." She didn't resist, but followed as he took her hand, tugged her to her feet, then led her into the bedroom.

"I'm not after sex, Angel. You've had a rough evening and I think you've got a little bit of shock going on. Let's just lie down and maybe get some rest and see how things are in the morning."

He peeled her shirt off, Ava moving on autopilot to let him get her ready for bed.

"You'll be gone tomorrow."

"What was that?"

"You'll be gone tomorrow. You have that thing with your club." She blinked but didn't follow his movements as he bustled around the bedroom getting them both ready for bed. The whole world seemed fuzzy and out of sorts.

Then Cowboy stopped in front of her, eased her down so she sat on the edge of the bed then sat beside her. When he cupped her face in both hands, her gaze went to his face, and she was able to focus on him.

"Angel, you had a rough day. It was more than a typical day and I'm not going to leave you until I know you're fine. If that means missing my ride, I'll miss the ride." He paused, his gaze searching her face. "I already let Deke know. He'll lead tomorrow. I'll make sure you're okay and that we're okay." His gaze dropped and he shook his head before looking back up at her. "I don't know how it happened so fast, but I've fallen for you. Hard. I love you and there is no way I'm going to leave you on your own to process something like this. Understand?"

It wasn't until his thumb swept across her cheek that Ava realized she was crying.

"I love you too. I was afraid I was being stupid and the only one who could fall so fast."

"You're not stupid and you're not alone. I'm not sure where things will go from here. But we'll figure it out...If you're game?" He seemed to watch her for any sign she was ready to walk away.

"I'm game. I've lived more in the last week with you than I did in fifteen years with Hank. I feel more for you now that I ever felt for him." Ava threw her arms around Cowboy's neck and buried her face against his chest.

All the pent-up emotion from the ordeal of being kidnapped go. She sobbed against his chest. She couldn't help but fall a little harder in love when his arms came around her. He murmured comforting words into the top of her head and let her cry. When she was finished, he tucked her into bed and curled up next to her, one arm wrapped tight around her.

This was how it should be. This was how a relationship should feel. Safe, comfortable, and loved.

Thank you for reading Cowboy, part of the Ride with Me series. Please consider leaving a review on your favorite retailer.

If you're looking for more from Melissa Stevens please consider joining
her VIP reader list for weekly updates on what she's working on now, as well as specials, giveaways and more.

All of her works can be found on her website at http://melissastevens.us

.

9 798224 246175